Dr CASSWELL'S STUDENT

by

SARAH FISHER

CHIMERA

Dr Casswell's Student published by
Chimera Publishing Ltd
PO Box 152
Waterlooville
Hants
PO8 9FS

Printed and bound in Great Britain by
Omnia Books Ltd, Glasgow

Dr CASSWELL's STUDENT

Sarah Fisher

'By God, you are a temptress, girl. You have the body of a whore and the face of an angel,' he muttered thickly, wiping his lips. 'That old devil Orme at the Abbey said you would serve me well, and he was right. But you need to be taught who is master here and who the slave; unbroken you are far too heady a drug.'

From beside his bed he pulled out a thin whip, the ornate handle set with jet. 'I used this to break my favourite horse. How fitting that I should use it next on you.'

When I saw the whip I began to struggle anew and cried out in protest. I would do whatever he asked. There was no need to beat me; wasn't I already at his mercy?

Chapter One

Sarah Morgan closed the door of her car and looked up at Doctor Casswell's country house. Moonlight picked its way between skeletal trees, reflecting in the windows of the mansion, giving them the appearance of cold unseeing eyes. On the lake below the terrace a chill autumn wind stirred the oily black water into life. She shivered and pulled her coat up around her shoulders, wondering if it had been a mistake to accept the doctor's offer of extra work.

In the three months since she had taken up the post as clerical assistant at Heally End Museum they had barely spoken – so the invitation to help with his research had come as a complete surprise. Sarah was flattered too, and more than a little curious about her enigmatic employer.

Ahead of her the arched front door opened and a wedge of light cut across the unkempt drive way.

'Miss Morgan? Is that you?'

Sarah struggled to find her voice; she had become increasingly nervous driving along the narrow lanes towards Doctor Casswell's country estate. Miles from anywhere, without a village or even a road sign to follow once she had turned off the main road, her imagination had got the better of her. Now, hearing his familiar cultured voice in the darkness she felt foolish. Struggling to regain her composure, Sarah called, 'Good evening, Doctor Casswell. I'm so sorry I'm late – I'd no idea you lived so far from town.'

Framed in the doorway, caught in silhouette, the doctor seemed taller and more imposing than she remembered him, though what she noticed most clearly was the moonlight reflecting in his dark eyes. He beckoned her closer.

'You're here now. Come in and get warm. Leave the keys in the car. I'll have one of the servants collect your luggage.' His voice was flat, devoid of emotion.

Sarah hurried up the steps, eager to be out of the bitter night wind. Her host waved her inside, and almost instantly the sense of apprehension returned.

The enormous baronial hall of Casswell House was lit by a single bare bulb dangling from a flex in the centre of the ceiling. Rather than illuminate the hall the circle of jaundiced light seemed only to emphasis its brooding gloom. Above them the vaulted ceilings reached up into the shadows. On the panelled walls, oil paintings – dark portraits that echoed of Doctor Casswell's hawkish features – stared down at her.

As Sarah glanced around, Doctor Casswell indicated that she should follow him. 'You will be working in my study,' he said. 'It's warmer in there.'

From the shadows a small Oriental man appeared. The doctor waved him towards the open front door. 'Chang, take Miss Morgan's luggage up to her room.' He glanced back at Sarah. 'I thought we would eat supper while we work, if you have no objection.'

It appeared that any social niceties she might have expected had already been dispensed with. Then again, Sarah decided, looking up into the faces of Casswell's aristocratic forebears, it was obvious that the doctor thought of her merely as an employee – a lesser mortal –

rather than a social equal. Perhaps she had been naïve to expect anything more.

In contrast to the hall, Casswell's study was quite cosy. A cheery fire burnt in the grate, and the central desk was illuminated by a large lamp. The walls were lined with books. To the left of the fire was a smaller desk on which stood a word processor, and beside that was a display case in which rested a small open book. Sarah, without thinking, stared down at the manuscript. The pages, no bigger than a child's hand, were covered in carefully written script, formed in tiny precise letters.

Sarah heard the doctor close the heavy door.

'So, this is it?' she said in a respectful whisper.

'No.' Casswell shook his head. 'This is just a single page facsimile, bound to resemble the complete work. The original is safe in the vault. I would like to remind you again, Miss Morgan, of the need for complete and utter secrecy about this project. Until I have completed the translation of the whole document and the laboratory returns the tests on the fabric of the book, details of its contents, even of its existence, must not leave this house. Is that perfectly clear? It is imperative that I have the opportunity to establish the manuscript's authenticity undisturbed by any outside attention – or any other interested parties. As we agreed, I've arranged a leave of absence with the museum for you. The trustees fully understand the significance of the work, so there won't be a problem there.'

Sarah nodded. 'Of course, doctor. Is the material politically sensitive?'

To her surprise her employer laughed, though the sound was not warm, nor did it make her feel any more at ease. 'It is most definitely sensitive, Miss Morgan,' he said in a strange uneven tone. 'Now, if you would care to take a look through the notes I've already made,' he indicated a loose-leaf folder on the desk. 'I will have Chang bring in supper for you.'

Sarah took off her coat and settled herself at the desk, and was about to ask the Doctor how he would like the transcripts to be set out when she realised she was already alone. Somewhat bemused, Sarah turned to the first page of the notes and began to read:

...My body aches from the application of the lash and my breasts and their buds, sweet cherries, are bruised and crushed from my master's rough handling. If I close my eyes I can still imagine his muscular body above me, his manhood thrusting deep inside my sex, whilst his fingers twist and nip at my most delicate flesh.

My head aches from the ocean of tears I have shed tonight. Yet, as I lay here alone on my narrow bed, listening to the musicians playing in the hall below – there is a banquet being held in my lady's honour – amongst the sense of pain and humiliation another flame burns almost as bright; a desire so dark and unholy that I can give it no name.

Between my legs I can still feel the remnants of my master's seed mingling with the bright blood of my lost maidenhood...

Sarah gasped in surprise and felt her face redden. Glancing over her shoulder, she was relieved now that Doctor Casswell had left her alone to study the opening pages. Who could have written such an account, and why? Her gaze dropped once again to the doctor's notes, her mind absorbing the intensely erotic passages carefully recorded in his fluid intricate hand:

...I believe now that I understand exactly what my role at the Castle is to be, not as my mentor, Father Orme, had led me to believe, as teacher to my master's children, but as his chattel, his slave, his concubine. My body is his to control and use as he wishes, and it is my sincere belief that Father Orme knew all along what my fate here was to be.

Since I arrived from the Abbey I have often noticed the way my lord has looked at me, the kindness he has paid me, the warm words and gentle manner of our dealings. Many times I have observed him watching me while I have been teaching the children, and thought him an attentive and caring father. But no more. Now I know it was not a father's pride nor a gentleman's courtesy to an uncertain and nervous girl that has fuelled his actions, but a ploy to gain my trust.

This evening he called me to his chamber, just as the daylight was beginning to fade. The Lady Elizabeth has returned home this day from a three month pilgrimage to the shrine of St Arnot, and there is much celebration in the house. Every torch has been lit, the house is alive with activity, and a great feast has been prepared for her homecoming. The air is heavy with the scent of rich food and herbs, and I, along with the rest of the household, was to be decked out in all my finery. I wore my best green gown with the finest braids and had plaited ribbons in my hair for the celebrations.

When my lord's servant summoned me I thought he would have me read awhile, before dining, as has been his custom since my arrival, but instead when I reached his chambers he handed me a goblet of mulled wine.

'Here, girl,' he said, a strange expression in his eyes. 'Let us drink a hearty toast to my lady's homecoming.'

I took the goblet he handed me and drank deeply, as was his request. I offered my congratulations on his wife's safe return but he waved my words away. The wine was strong and I'd had little opportunity to eat all day. It made my head spin, and as I passed him the goblet back he caught hold of my wrist and, pulling me towards him, kissed me hard. I was astonished and jerked away in horror.

Before I could protest he asked me who I considered to be my master. I wondered if he had supped too much wine, and said quickly, 'Why you, sir. You know I am pledged to serve you and your family.'

He nodded and seemed appeased. 'And you are loyal to my house?'

I nodded, wondering where his questions would lead. He knows full well the circumstances of my engagement at the castle. Although from a good family I was orphaned as a small child and brought up and educated by the church. I have been promised in service to his Lordship's household as recompense for the charitable contributions from the castle estates to the Abbey.

His eyes darkened. 'I will have you then, girl – as proof of the loyalty you show me.'

I thought I had misunderstood his meaning. 'Have me, sir?' I repeated nervously.

He looked liked a wolf, eyes narrow and cruel. 'Are you deaf, girl? Is it that you don't understand what is said to you or is it that you are stupid? Take off your pretty new gown, little church mouse, and let me look at what the good priest has sold to me. Or would you deny me the prize I have already paid for?'

'I am a maiden, sir, a virgin,' I said, frightened now and anxious to end our encounter. I had never seen him so hot-blooded or so frightening.

He grinned, running the back of his hand over his lips, wiping away the remnants of the wine. 'All the better, lady, all the better. I will teach you how a maid should truly serve her man. I have a hunger for a little fresh meat. Now, take off your gown and let me see my prize.'

I hurried back towards the door and caught hold of the handle, only to discover it was locked fast.

His expression hardened. 'Come along, girl, I have neither the time nor the patience to play games with you. Do as I ask and do it quickly.'

'But surely your wife awaits you, sir,' I protested in desperation.

He snorted. 'How naïve you are. Wife in name only now, sweet child. Surely you know that ours was marriage drawn up to join two quarrelling factions – a marriage of dynastic importance but no love, lady, no passion. Do you think I would have chosen a woman fifteen years my senior had I been given the choice? Now do as I command, or will you make me take, by force, what was promised me?'

There was no escape. He watched me struggling with the door, unmoved by my pleas for mercy, his expression hard and cold. Finally it was obvious he had no intention of letting me go, and I could see no other course than to do as he ordered. Slowly I undid the fastenings of my robe and let it drop to the floor.

His eyes burned like coals as he took in the details of my undress. Tears formed in my eyes, tears of shame and fear, but he was not content. He waved me to continue, his lips set in a narrow line and then – as I began to fumble with the ribbons of my petticoats – he fell upon me with an angry roar of frustration, ripping away the thin fabric with rough and frantic hands.

I fought as hard as I could to resist him, but he was unstoppable, and even then some dark part of my soul knew that I relished his attentions. Some part of me understood his desire, and it both excited and appalled me. The material gave way under his eager fingers and he threw me down onto the cold hard floor.

Stunned, I could barely breath as roughly he turned me onto my back, my colour rising along with my shame as his hands eagerly explored my nakedness.

In my distress I wondered whether his attentions were some cruel ungodly reward for my unclean thoughts about him. Since my arrival at the castle I had come to consider him a handsome and desirable man. He has often come to me at night in my dreams, making me sweat like a mare on heat, my body aching for release. But surely I cannot be held responsible for those dark fantasies that come to tempt a sleeping mind? I have tried hard not to let my mind follow along this path when I am awake. After all, he is the lord of the house, married, and father of my lady's children. Even if I now know there is no love between them, they are still joined under God's law in the eyes of the church.

No bonded creature such as I would dare look so high in their affections, but perhaps he had already seen the base desire in my eyes? Perhaps it had angered him so much that he sought to punish me for my presumption?

He was once a soldier, and a powerfully built man. I was helpless to resist his advances, and my fighting and sobbing seemed to make him more and more excited. Finally, exhausted, I could fight no more and I surrendered, too terrified to do anything but wait, half naked, trembling and afraid, for him to do his worst.

Straddling me on the cold unforgiving flagstones he manhandled me as if I weighed no more than a sack of flour, stripping off every last shred of my petticoats. Grabbing hold of my arms he tied my wrists together with a rag and dragging me to my feet, secured them to the frame of his bed.

Catching hold of my chin he tipped my face up towards his. To my surprise my submission seemed to have pleased him. He smiled at me, though the smile did not warm his dark eyes.

'What a prize you are, sweet little Beatrice. I want you to understand that I am your master in all things. Your body, your very soul belongs to me now. Do you understand?'

I nodded. The tears of humiliation and fear trickled down my face.

He seemed happy with my response. 'Trust me, Beatrice, trust me and give yourself to me completely. Don't think I haven't noticed the way you look at me. So brazen – so ripe. I already know you are mine to command. Give yourself to me and I will not betray your trust. I will show you paradise.'

What could I say or do when he had me just as he wanted, tied and naked? My tears continued to flow like a river. He ran a hand over my flank as if I were a favoured dog or horse. Perhaps his touch was meant to quieten or comfort me, but by all the saints it felt to me like the hand of a man staking his claim to a new possession.

Such passion and pain he has shown me in just one evening. Once I was at his mercy his smooth hands cupped and squeezed my breasts. His mouth worked against mine, teeth biting down on my tongue and lips. And no matter how much I cried out and begged for clemency my pleas fell on deaf ears.

His touch both unnerved and excited me. At times he caressed me as I knew a lover should; gently, tenderly, tonguing the soft folds of my quim, and exploring my body as any good husband might. And then just as I glimpsed the lights of heaven, he stopped and pulled away.

'By God, you are a temptress, girl. You have the body of a whore and the face of an angel,' he muttered thickly, wiping his lips. 'That old devil Orme at the Abbey said you would serve me well, and he was right. But you need to be taught who is master here and who the slave; unbroken you are far too heady a drug.'

From beside his bed he pulled out a thin whip, the ornate handle set with jet. 'I used this to break my favourite horse. How fitting that I should use it next on you.'

When I saw the whip I began to struggle anew and cried out in protest. I would do whatever he asked. There was no need to beat me; wasn't I already at his mercy?

He ignored my cries, drew back the head of the whip, and lay on a stroke that took me to the very edge of consciousness. The whip's fiery tongue lit a raw red path across my flesh as hot as the sun itself. Every sinew of my body screamed out in complaint and in terror – but he would not be stopped.

I twisted away from him, desperate to avoid the whip's harsh lesson. But my master would not be denied. This time the fine leather snaked around my torso and bit into my belly and then my breasts, leaving a livid scar in its wake. By now I could scarcely hold a sane thought in my head. The only sound that filled my brain was that of the whip as it cracked out again and again. I have no idea how long he beat me, only that the blows seemed to go on longer than time itself. At last, when the air was still, I struggled to catch my breath.

With firm hands he cut me down and I tumbled forward into his arms. My breath came in raw gasps and my head spun. Great weals had lifted on my shoulders, back and breasts, and my throat and eyes were sore from crying out in pain and… and yet mingled with it all was an odd sense of pleasure that terrified me more than the pain itself.

But if I thought my ordeal was over I was much mistaken. My master picked me up in his strong arms and lay me down on the bed, his eyes alight with a lust that burned as bright as any star. Far from sating his hunger, my beating and humiliation had lit an unstoppable passion. As I cowered amongst the rich tumble of linen, eyes wide with terror, he unfastened his breeches. For the first time I saw his pillar of manhood, raised like an avenging sword from between the folds of the cloth.

I could hardly imagine that my tiny body would accommodate such a beast. Roughly he pulled me up onto my knees and pressed my head and lips towards his phallus. Afraid and repelled by what he demanded of me, I understood only to well what he craved. He pulled me closer still. Powerless to resist I kissed him humbly, keeping my eyes downcast, and then took his great throbbing sex into my mouth.

To my astonishment I found myself lost in the act of worshipping him; an ancient act of submission to his masculinity. Lapping at the great ivory shaft my body began to glow with desire, my sex wet and throbbing with an unfulfilled need.

Eagerly now I cupped him with my fingers, longing for some kind of climax to this dark game. As I began to find a rhythm, hands, lips and tongue working in harmony, his dark eyes flashed with fury; had he not already told me it was he who was the master and I the slave?

Pushing me back amongst the covers, he pressed forward. I knew then I was lost; his to command. There was a fragrant wetness that trickled from between my thighs; the same rich juices that flowed whenever I dreamt of my master.

He forced my legs apart with his knee and opening me cruelly with his fingers, guided his phallus home. For an instant my body resisted his assault, my sex tight and unbreached. There was a terrible raw surge of pain when I truly thought I might split apart as my body fought to hold him back, and then finally he drove his cock home and I cried out like an animal on a stormy night, hungry and wild and afraid.

To my amazement, as he began to move my body opened for him like a flower blooming. Rubbing against me, his hands working over my bruised breasts, I was astonished by the strange tendrils of pleasure that grew into intense spirals of light, twisting up from low inside my belly.

I thought perhaps the pain and the shame of the beating had driven me insane and these feelings were the divine rewards of my madness and obedience. Was this wild surging pleasure the very madness that would drown out the last remnants of reason?

Heat rose like a fever inside me until I thought I would die from sheer delight. And then, at the very pinnacle of pleasure when my demise seemed assured, I felt my master thrust forward once more, his shaft pulsating deep inside me, his passion a heady counterpoint to the waves of ecstasy that roared through me. And then, finally, there was stillness.

He pulled out of me and struggling to his feet, tidied his clothes.

'You will come whenever I call for you, Beatrice,' he said breathlessly. 'I will brook no excuses, girl, no delays. You are mine now, do you understand?'

I nodded, unable to find the words to reply, and clambered off the bed, collecting my gown and the torn remnants of my petticoats. As he unlocked the door he caught hold of my arm. His features had softened. His eyes, so steely before, were gentle now.

'Remember who you serve, lady. I am your only master. Our fates are closely entwined, Beatrice. Yours and mine.'

I do not understand what he means. All I know is that I am still expected to attend the feast, and my body and mind are in a raging tumult...

Sitting alone in Doctor Casswell's study, Sarah Morgan realised she was struggling to breath. The computer screen in front of her was completely blank; she hadn't typed a single word since beginning to read the manuscript. Its flickering unforgiving eye silently observed her discomfort. Her face was flushed, her body hot and feverish. She swallowed hard.

Why had Doctor Casswell asked her to type up his translation when he could have easily asked any of the other girls who worked in the office? They were far more efficient and competent typists than she was. Sarah realised, for the first time, that asking her to stay at his house made no sense at all. Was it, whispered a dark voice deep inside her mind, that the good doctor recognised the parallels in Sarah's life to the hapless Beatrice?

She shivered. Surely her mind was playing tricks on her. How could her situation possibly mirror the fate of the long dead slave girl? But even as her mind framed the question Sarah knew the similarities were there: wasn't she an orphan too, brought up by a great aunt? Although only twenty-two, hadn't she spent the last few years of her life caring for the old woman? Though hardly a convent, it was as close as it was possible to get in the modern world. And hadn't an old family friend found her the job at the museum once her aunt had gone into a home? An elderly male friend of the family who had known Casswell for years? Perhaps she, like Beatrice, had unwittingly been sold to her master. Sarah glanced nervously around the small study, wondering if it was too late to turn down Casswell's offer of extra work.

She jumped as the study door swung open to reveal the doctor's servant carrying a supper tray. The tiny Oriental man set the meal down on a side-table by the fire.

'If you ring the bell when you've finished, Miss Morgan, I will come and collect the tray,' he said flatly in impeccable English. 'And after you've eaten I will show you to your room.'

Sarah nodded. Her stomach rumbled in response to the appetising smell of the food. It crossed her mind that her imagination was getting the better of her. She was just hungry and nervous, that was all. Things would look different when she had eaten.

She smiled up at him. 'Thank you.'

He bowed in response.

As soon as he had left the room, but before she began to eat her supper, Sarah typed in a working title for the manuscript:

'The Diary of Beatrice', translated by Doctor R J Casswell.

Satisfied that she was back in control, Sarah Morgan turned her attentions to the tray.

Chapter Two

After supper Chang led Sarah upstairs to her bedroom. She felt better for having eaten. Abandoning the manuscript and the word processor, she followed the little Oriental man back into the hall. Stepping out of the warm study she wondered again whether accepting the invitation to Casswell House had been such a good idea. Since he had first shown her to the office there had been no other sign of the doctor. With just Chang for company the old house seemed dark and cold and foreboding. The oppressive gloom made the hairs lift on the back of Sarah's neck.

The sweeping staircase was lit by dusty lamps and bare bulbs. The whole place had obviously seen much better days; the carpets were threadbare, the drapes faded and thin. Even in the poor light it was impossible to ignore the layers of dust and cobwebs that clung to every surface. Here and there pieces of plaster had fallen off the walls revealing the lathe below.

So Sarah was surprised when Chang opened an ornate door on the second floor to reveal a warm comfortable room. A large coal fire burned in the grate. The hearth was flanked by two arm-winged chairs, while lamps on side-tables lit the room with a soft golden glow. Opposite the door, floor-length curtains framed a dramatic view out over the grounds, and standing in the bay window was a *chaise longue*, upholstered in black velvet and strewn with cream silk cushions. On the dressing table stood a bowl of fresh flowers. It certainly wasn't the kind of room Sarah had been expecting.

Through an open door she could see into the bathroom, where plush white towels hung from a rail. But what really caught and held her attention was the enormous mirror that dominated the main room. It stretched from floor to ceiling on the wall opposite the bed.

The ornate gilt frame would have looked ridiculous in a smaller room or a lesser house. It was surmounted by two huge plump cherubs and from the baskets they carried, tumbled a cornucopia of fruit, flowers, birds and animals, and a tumult of bubbling water and twisted ribbons that made up the frame.

In the mirror's cool reflection the huge bed was caught and held like an exquisite picture.

Sarah glanced at the bed's carved wooden uprights and for an instant imagined Beatrice tied there, naked and afraid, awaiting her master's pleasure. The image sent an intense electric pulse of desire down her spine, making her shiver.

Behind her Chang watched, his face expressionless as she hastily ordered her thoughts. 'I hadn't imagined I'd be staying anywhere so luxurious,' she said.

The servant bowed curtly. 'I will tell the doctor that the room is satisfactory. I have unpacked your things,' he said, indicating the wardrobe and tallboy. 'Breakfast is at eight.'

Sarah thanked him and then added, 'Do you think it would be all right to bring Doctor Casswell's notes up here to read? I thought I could begin transcribing them tomorrow.'

Chang's expression didn't change. 'I will ask the doctor.'

As he turned to leave, Sarah continued. 'Will I see Doctor Casswell again this evening? I mean, does he expect me to go downstairs? I thought perhaps he might want me to spend the...' her voice faded under the man's unwavering stare. She wasn't sure what it was that Casswell expected of her, but as it was barely eight o'clock she hadn't considered the possibility that Chang could be showing her up to bed.

The servant looked surprised. 'Doctor Casswell usually spends his evenings alone. He works or reads. I do not think he anticipates you joining him this evening, Miss Morgan. Would you like me to ask him?'

Sarah shook her head; it seemed she was dismissed, unless of course the doctor assumed she would want to continue working until bedtime. She smiled at Chang and then waved him away. 'Thank you. It was a long drive; I think I'll just get settled in.'

The little man nodded. 'If you want anything, please ring.' He indicated a bell-pull beside the mantelpiece and then closed the door quietly behind him. As soon as he was gone, Sarah let out a sigh of relief and slumped into one of the winged chairs by the fire. Working at Casswell Hall was going to be far more difficult than she imagined. The house and its surroundings were so strange. The Doctor made her nervous – even with Chang she was on tenterhooks – and then there was the content of the manuscript itself.

She glanced around the room. Chang had already unpacked her possessions: her books – two novels – lay on the bedside cabinet, clothes, shoes, everything – even her toiletries, were neatly arranged in the appropriate places. On a tray by the fire were refreshments: bottles of wines and spirits, soft drinks, tea and coffee, suggesting that she was expected to stay in her room when not working downstairs.

Exploring the large room she suddenly felt more like a prisoner than a guest, and it seemed odd to catch sight of herself in the huge mirror as she crossed its path. When, a few minutes later, Chang returned with the Doctor's notes, she couldn't help but wonder if the little man knew exactly what the book contained.

As he closed the door, she opened a bottle of wine and poured herself a glass, pulled the chair closer to the fire and switched on a lamp. It took no more than a few seconds for the images of Beatrice and the servant girl's brooding master to fill Sarah's thoughts. What perturbed her more than the vivid imagery was that in her mind's eye it was Doctor Casswell who laid on the whip – and her own body that waited for its cruel kiss.

Hastily Sarah closed her eyes, trying to block out the fleeting but intense fantasy. She glanced down at the innocent looking folder on her lap. In a sense it was like holding Pandora's box. Perhaps it would be foolish to open it again and immerse herself in the world of Beatrice and her newly discovered passions.

As if her fingers had a life of their own she opened the book and began to read:

...I am lost and I realise now that there is no one left for me to turn to for help. Today my master's servant, Arturo de Vallon, summoned me from my duties. Leaving the children with the maid I hurried through the castle to my master's apartments. This is the first time he has called me since the night of my Lady Elizabeth's feast and I was afraid and excited by turns. Imagine my surprise when I got to his chambers only to discover that they were empty.

I turned to ask Arturo whether my master had left any instructions to meet him elsewhere, and then I saw the look in the serving man's eyes. He grinned and shook his head. 'Not a-one. The master is away this morning bringing the yearlings homes. So, there's just you and I, girl, and I intend to sample a little of what the master enjoyed so well.' He paused, eyes bright with lust. 'I was outside last time and heard the kiss of the whip, and found myself a place where I could watch. I saw how you bucked and twisted beneath him, how you lifted up that sweet shameless body of yours and drew him deep into your ripe quim.'

Arturo picked up a flagon from the table and drank deeply. 'The master and I go back a long way. He on a noble path and I, until now, his faithful man-at-arms. He has never begrudged me anything from his table. I often sup of his wine, eat alongside him just as if we were brothers, not man and master – and now I will have a little of his pleasure.'

I had been slowly backing away while Arturo was speaking. As he lifted the flagon again I turned and ran towards the door, but to my horror he seemed to have anticipated my move and leapt ahead of me, the flagon and its contents exploding across the floor as he slammed the door shut.

Grabbing me by the arms he spun me around and kissed me hard, his breath foul and pungent. As his lips met mine he drove me hard back against the wall, banging my head. I shrieked out in pain and fear, the darkness closing over me, but he was oblivious to my injury. Snatching up a rag from the side-tables he tied it around my mouth so that I shouldn't scream out again and renewed his assault, his fingers fighting with the fastenings of my bodice. I struggled furiously, trying hard to break away, but he was having none of it and held me tight with one great fist.

Once my breasts were ripped free he toyed with them, twisting my nipples between his coarse fingers, grunting and slavering like a wild animal, spittle trickling down onto his chin as he sucked and bit on their sensitive peaks.

Pinning me back against the wall he pushed his foot between mine, forcing my legs apart, and while with one hand he squeezed and nipped at my breasts, his other hand gathered up the folds of my skirt, seeking entry into my most secret places. He towered over me, his rancid breath hot and wet on my skin – and as he leered down at me, body pressed hard against mine, I was too afraid to move.

Just in the instant when I thought all was lost, the inner door leading into my master's private chapel opened, and there stood none other than Father Orme, my mentor and teacher. This is the man who had engaged me to my master's household. My heart swelled with relief; surely he would not see me violated by this lewd villain.

'What goes on here, Arturo?' snapped Orme furiously, as the servant froze with me pinned to the wall, breasts exposed, his hand still forced up between my legs.

'Well,' the serving man began, reddening furiously 'I... I...'

To my horror, instead of ordering him to unhand me, Orme grinned at Arturo's obvious discomfort. 'No need to explain, man, I can see for myself. Taking a little ride on the master's filly, are we, while his lordship is busy elsewhere, eh?'

My cheeks flared crimson and I began to struggle once more in earnest. Orme gave me an icy look. 'Perhaps you would like me to hold her still so you can get mounted up more easily?'

Arturo grinned in disbelief. 'Most obliged, father,' he said, and turned me round, driving me back towards Orme so hard he winded me. The old man wrapped his arms tight around my waist. I could hardly believe what was happening. The old priest leant closer and pressed his face close to my hair, breathing in the scent of my body.

'Do exactly as you are told, girl,' he hissed as he kicked my legs apart. 'Arturo is a valuable ally. Did your Master not explain to you that it is your duty to give yourself to those who demand it? He has already told me how brazen you are, Beatrice, how wicked you are; temptation itself entrapping the poor unwary traveller.'

Any other words were lost as Arturo dragged my skirt up around my waist and sank to his knees before me. His tongue plunged into my quim and to my horror Orme's hands lifted to toy with my breasts. I could not resist them both and the filthy gag stopped me from calling out in protest.

Despite my humiliation and shame I also knew that I could not fight the dark spiral of pleasure that Arturo's tongue brought to life between my legs.

I began to writhe with pleasure, horrified by my body's eager submission to Arturo's explorations. Just as the first waves of pleasure rolled through me, Arturo clambered to his feet, and with Orme taking my weight, drove the head of his meaty purple phallus deep inside me.

The sensation of him working it deep made me gasp in

surprise. I could offer no resistance. My body opened like shimmering gossamer for his cock, and then once he was fully home, it closed around him eagerly, hungrily, like a clenched fist.

Perhaps the old priest was right – perhaps I was as wicked as he suggested. The fierce thrusting of Arturo's body against mine lit a beacon fire deep inside my mind and I was dragged helplessly by this sweating grunting serving man deep into the raging seas of oblivion. Deep inside me I felt his cock throbbing. Seconds later he slithered from the confines of my body and was quickly dismissed by Father Orme.

The old priest let go of me and I dropped to my knees, overcome by shame and the dizzy echoes of my passion.

'Stay exactly as you are,' snapped Orme, as I began to tidy my clothes. I reddened, only too aware of the creamy swell of my naked breasts, my nipples still flushed and hard from their rough caresses. Even now between my legs I could feel the serving man's seed trickling slowly onto my thighs.

'I thought I could trust you Beatrice to use your learning to good effect. This is how you repay my faith, is it?' said Father Orme in an icy tone. 'Using your wiles to seduce your master and his servants, and flaunting your nakedness before a respectable man of the cloth?'

I blushed furiously, and pulling away the cloth gag began to protest my innocence, but Orme held up his hand to silence me. 'Don't try and defend yourself you little slut. I know exactly how to punish you kind for your brazen and unseemly behaviour, Beatrice. I will take it upon myself to take on your correction before you lose your very soul to this madness. Lift your petticoats. I will beat this lewdness from you.'

Crouched on all fours, I braced myself as he ran a hand over my backside. He pushed my thin petticoats aside so I was completely exposed for his explorations. I blushed furiously, imagining the picture I presented. My flesh still bore the marks of my lord's horsewhip, and Orme grunted his approval. 'I see the master has already begun to train you... good... good.'

To my surprise his fingers worked down over my reddened buttocks to explore the sopping folds of my quim. He dipped inside me, grunting his appreciation, and then he slid a hand up over my belly and cupped my breasts so that the juices of my sex were smeared on my skin and nipples. The air seemed to be suffused with the heady scent of my excitement and Arturo's seed and, as Orme nipped at my flesh, without thinking I moaned with a mixture of delight and embarrassment.

The old priest growled furiously. 'I fear you are lost already, Beatrice. You are truly a whore. You need to be punished for such forwardness.'

Glancing back over my shoulder I realised he had removed the belt from his robe, and before I could move or compose myself, the broad leather strap exploded across my bare buttocks, making me shriek out in horror.

The heat and pain roared through my body like a storm wind. Still so close to the moments of pleasure, my skin seemed more sensitive and more delicate than normal, and I wept and screamed at the intensity of the pain from Orme's beating. And yet... and yet... amongst it all was a tendril of desire, so dark, so unholy that it unnerved me.

When the beating had finished I instinctively moved closer to my tormentor, cowering at his feet, silently begging his forgiveness and his absolution.

As I rested my head against his thigh I was aware of his manhood pressing forward, seeking attention between the folds of his coarse robes. He looked down at me, eyes as bright as ice, and without a word I parted his robes and pressed my lips to his gnarled cock, my hands lifting to cradle the distended bulk of his balls and stroke at his engorged shaft. He shivered and closed his eyes. With one hand he brushed the hair back from my face and then thrust forward, cursing himself for his own weakness and desires as he did so.

It was a matter of moments, no more, before I tasted his excitement and an instant later a great fountain of warm frothing seed filled my mouth – so copious a quantity that it coursed out onto my chin and dripped down over my breasts. Orme sighed as if I had relieved him of a great burden.

He ran a finger down through the trail of his pleasure where it clung to my flesh. 'Go back to your work,' he whispered in a thick unnatural voice. 'I need to be alone for a while.'...

In the darkened room that stood behind the two-way mirror looking into Sarah's bedroom, Doctor Rigel Casswell poured another brandy and settled back in his armchair. By moving a little it was possible to see almost all the interior of Sarah Morgan's room.

He watched her now, though she was totally unaware of his presence. Seated by the fire she drained her wine glass, closed the folder containing his notes and very slowly got to her feet. Her eyes were glassy, her breath shallow and excited. She moved with a nervous grace as if she was uncertain what was expected of her even when she was alone. There was a rather unworldly look about

Sarah Morgan; an air of innocence and naïvety he'd noticed on the very first day she had commenced working at the museum. They were qualities that both excited and delighted him.

Rigel Casswell was a patient man. Like a hunter he knew the importance of understanding his prey, to observe and understand its habits, all the better to trap it – to tame it. It had taken him months to plan Sarah Morgan's seduction and find a way to persuade her to join him at Casswell Hall – but he already knew it would be well worth the effort.

In the bedroom Sarah picked up her dressing gown from the foot of the bed and padded barefoot towards the bathroom. At the door she hesitated and turned to glance into the mirror.

He could see the flame of desire burning in her eyes. He knew she was excited by what she had read, and frustrated that the passion could not be fulfilled. As if hypnotised by her own reflection Sarah stepped closer to the glass, hands moving almost subconsciously over her body.

Who, Casswell wondered, did she imagine was caressing her? Was it the dissolute Father Orme? Or the Lord of the Castle? Or perhaps the rough hands of his manservant, Arturo? Casswell wished he could be privy to her secret thoughts; could tap into the well-spring of her desire.

Slowly the girl began to undress. Like a moth drawn to a candle flame she was caught helplessly by the mirror's unblinking eye. First she unfastened her jacket, dropping it onto the ottoman at the foot of the bed, and then one by one undid the buttons of her crisp white cotton blouse. Shamelessly now she stared into the mirror, eyes dark with desire, caught up by the power of her own image.

How vain, how brazen Sarah Morgan could be when alone, thought Casswell. She would soon learn to be humble in his presence; a slave, a handmaiden to his desire, just like the beautiful Beatrice de Fleur.

Casswell leant forward, watching as the thin blouse fell silently to the floor. Sarah's breasts were exquisitely shaped and generously full, cradled in a delicate white lace bra that barely covered her large pink nipples. Gently, almost lovingly, she cupped one in her palm, thumb and finger caressing the rapidly hardening peak.

Casswell held his breath, amazed at Sarah's behaviour. He certainly hadn't expected her to be so bold or so ripe with desire. He smiled thinly, sensing a delightful thread of self-consciousness still present, mingling with her obvious need for satisfaction. Cheeks tinged with pink, eyes bright with excitement, Sarah Morgan's exquisite body was more than he could possibly have hoped for.

Slowly now she unfastened her bra and posed for a second or two, absorbing the erotic potential of her reflection before undoing the zip of her skirt and pushing it to the carpet. Her waist was narrow, her hips full and womanly, her belly softly rounded with an almost peach-like blush to it. Her skirt and underwear seemed to have been discarded in one sweeping movement. She turned to admire herself in profile, while her fingertips eagerly outlined a trail down over her breasts and belly. Her nipples were hard as cherry pits, her whole body suffused with a bloom of desire.

Casswell drained his glass, imagining Sarah bound and tied for his pleasure. He could easily visualise her struggling against her restraints, those pert breasts thrust forward, perspiration trickling between them in crystal droplets. He could hear her cry out as the whip bit into that lush, ripe flesh, her mouth open, eyes wide with fear and desire.

Through the looking-glass he watched as Sarah flexed her hips, revealing a tantalising glimpse of her sex; a pink, moist exotic flower that begged for his attention. It was trimmed by a corona of dark shiny curls, and as he watched Sarah artfully slid a finger between the heavy outer lips.

Casswell closed his eyes for an instant, imagining the sensation of her sweet body moving against and around his. Her seduction and education would be pure joy – she was so ready. Leaning closer it was almost as if he could smell her through the cool glass. Like Beatrice, Sarah would have to learn and understand who was master and who slave. As yet unaware of her power and her raw sexuality, she would be better once he had broken her in; taught her what he expected and needed from her.

Through the mirror Casswell could see that Sarah's busy fingers had found the pleasure bud that nestled deep within those fragrant lips. He sensed it was time to act. He got to his feet and moved towards the door with Chang, who was no more than a step or two behind him.

When he stepped into Sarah's room he saw the strange mixture of shock and excitement on her face. She stepped away from the mirror, frantically reaching for her clothes, stunned and deeply embarrassed at being caught in so vulnerable and so seductive a state.

'Stand still,' he ordered in a voice that brooked no contradiction. She froze, her hands outstretched.

'What do you want?' she whispered.

Casswell smiled thinly. 'Oh come, come, you're not unintelligent, Miss Morgan, surely you already know the answer to that? You must have guessed why I invited you here. You are my Beatrice.'

She stepped away from him, eyes bright with fear and excitement.

'No,' she murmured, although they both knew it was a lie. Her tone was uneven and yet her fear had made her less conscious of her nakedness. There was a definite air of defiance about her stance. How delightful, thought Casswell. What a pleasure it would be to train such a beautiful, strong-willed creature. 'You're mistaken,' she continued.

'I am?' he said and turned away, feigning indifference. 'What a terrible shame. In that case I won't waste any more of your time. You may leave now, my dear. Tonight. I really have no desire to keep you here against your will. Chang will pack for you.'

He saw something flash across Sarah's eyes and then he extended a hand in invitation. 'Or perhaps you might like to reconsider? Tell me honestly that you weren't excited by Beatrice's seduction? Tell me that some part of you did not tremble with delight as you imagined the kiss of the whip or the cut of the belt on her ripe and eager flesh. Tell me, Sarah… tell me. Tell me why you are naked in front of the mirror seeking solitary satisfaction?'

To his delight Sarah Morgan flushed scarlet and looked down.

Rigel Casswell knew then that Sarah was his. It would take time for her to understand what he truly wanted from her, but she had taken that first step towards embracing her true nature.

He nodded to Chang, who caught hold of Sarah's arm. Her instinctive reaction was to pull away.

Casswell shook his head. 'Don't fight the need that courses through your veins, Miss Morgan. I can see it in your eyes. Chang will prepare you for me.'

Sarah stared at him, and then without protest let Chang lead her into the bathroom.

Chapter Three

Hardly able to believe what was happening to her, Sarah felt as if she had stepped into some sort of dark compelling dream. There was a sense of unreality; lust and fear were a heady mixture. She could feel her pulse racing while she waited for the Oriental man to reveal what was to follow.

His face was an impassive mask as he moved around the room, silent and apparently unmoved by either her nakedness or her vulnerability. Sarah felt a ripple of apprehension. Chang opened the door to the shower cubicle and then turned towards her. From his pocket he produced a pair of soft leather manacles linked by several inches of fine chain. He held out his hand towards her – the gesture was an invitation not a command – although everything about his demeanour suggested this was not an invitation she could easily refuse.

Without thinking she stepped closer. It seemed that since Doctor Casswell had stepped into her bedroom her body was moving with a will of its own, as if Beatrice de Fleur's desire was fuelling her compliance. She wondered where this side of her nature had been hidden until now. Was Beatrice's diary the key that had unlocked this secret part of her?

Chang touched her and broke the chain of thought. Quickly, as if afraid she might change her mind, he slipped a leather strap over each wrist, jerking them tight before buckling them closed. She gasped with surprise as the leather bit into her flesh.

'Turn around and lift your arms above your head,' he ordered. Glancing up, she saw that set into the tiles above the shower head was a hook on an adjustable stem. It struck her then that she was not the first houseguest to have succumbed to Doctor Casswell's erotic invitation, but did as she was told. The servant's cool hands settled on her slim hips and lifted a little so the chain between the manacles caught over the hook and secured her for whatever might follow.

Sarah closed her eyes and swallowed hard. She had never felt or been so vulnerable in her life, and the sensation sent adrenaline surging through her veins like a burning fuse.

The white marble tiles were icy cool as they brushed against her spine. As Chang let go, the muscles in her arms screamed out in protest at being asked to take the weight of her body. She flinched while, very gently, Chang lowered the hook a little so the balls of her feet rested on the floor… and then he pulled her closer. For the first time she had a chance to look deep into the glacial darkness of his eyes.

'You will learn now what it really feels like to be tied like an animal waiting for your master's pleasure,' he said without emotion. 'You will soon understand that you are a slave, like Beatrice, a creature created purely for pleasure. It will be better if you accept your fate and learn the lessons now. It will be much easier.'

Sarah shivered. From his jacket Chang drew a broad strip of what looked liked chamois leather. When Sarah realised that he intended to blindfold her with it, she pulled away and started to protest.

The small man shook his head; it was pointless to resist.

What could she do or say to make him stop? She had a feeling her begging would only excite him. He would blindfold her with or without her co-operation, and the results would be the same.

For an instant Sarah felt a bright plume of fear rising from deep in her belly; she was totally helpless to resist either Chang or his master. The implications of the game she had agreed to play hit home as the Oriental reached up and knotted the leather firmly around her eyes. It clung tight like a second skin, moulding itself across the contours of her face, plunging her into complete darkness.

Sarah's reaction was to pull away from Chang, but it was pointless. She could do nothing other than await whatever was in store. For a few seconds all she could hear was the frantic beat of her pulse, and then there was a hiss and a deluge of water; icy cold and as sharp as needles, and then gradually getting warmer. As the torrent exploded across her skin she cried out, feeling faint as the water poured down over her, the sheer force of it making her gasp for breath.

She strained against her restraints, every nerve ending alight, her mind trying to reach beyond the darkness of the mask into the bathroom to guess what it was the two men had planned for her. After a moment or two the water slowed to a trickle and two hands began to work over her flesh; competent hands that coolly explored every inch as they soaped her.

'Open you legs,' Chang ordered.

Sarah did as she was told, only too aware of her vulnerability. The next thing she felt was a hand lathering the soft mount of her sex, followed by an odd sweeping motion, and a rasping sound. She held her breath, waiting for another stroke to confirm her fears. It came after a second or two and was followed by the terrifying but inescapable knowledge that the cool bite was a razor shaving away the corona of hair around her sex. She froze, too terrified to move and almost too terrified to breathe.

Chang was skilled in his work, and Rigel Casswell always enjoyed watching his girls being made ready. Sarah Morgan's preparations were of particular interest to him; he had every reason to believe she was still a virgin – and the idea both delighted and excited him. Certainly her lithe body had an exquisitely unsullied quality that was a joy to behold. He almost regretted that it was Chang who had the pleasure of touching her first.

The Oriental had stripped to the waist to attend to Sarah, his compact and sleekly muscled body, honed from marshal arts training, was a stunning contrast to Sarah's pale curves.

From beneath the blindfold a few tendrils of dark hair had formed into ringlets that framed her pretty face. A stray curl clung to her cheek, emphasising her open mouth and its full pink lips. Her tongue was visible as she struggled to control her breathing. Her breasts were covered in water droplets that glittered like crystals as she moved, her nipples as hard and dark as summer fruits.

Casswell imagined the heat of Sarah's skin, wet and slick beneath Chang's knowing fingertips, and shivered with pure pleasure. As he watched, the little Oriental parted Sarah's long legs, trimming away the last traces of pubic hair.

Casswell nodded his approval; enhanced by the line of her hip bones and the soft rise of her belly, Sarah's naked sex looked as pink and ripe as a fresh peach. Chang's fingers retraced the path of the razor, gently outlining the sensitive contours of the outer lips. Sarah's instinctive response was to move with his touch and moan softly.

Casswell smiled; like Beatrice de Fleur, beneath the innocent unsullied exterior the girl was wanton. And, like Beatrice, Sarah would be all the better when she was broken. Chang glanced in Casswell's direction. The Oriental's expression was totally devoid of emotion. Casswell often wondered at the exact nature of the thoughts behind those jet-black eyes. He knew it was a mistake to believe that Chang was untouched by the passion, the pleasure, and the pain, his fingertips unleashed.

Chang lifted the shower head down and rinsed away the last of the remaining foam from Sarah's body. The water pressure was strong enough to part the lips of the girl's sex and course down over her pleasure bud. The Oriental played the water back and forth making the girl shiver with pure delight; it was sweet torture.

Sarah began to move in time with the hypnotic movements, her hips following the stream of water as if they were connected to the glittering arc. She was straining forward now, eager to enjoy its watery caresses. Her excitement was rising rapidly. Casswell could see Chang had sensed it too, and just as the girl thrust her hips towards him, he turned the water off.

Casswell could sense her disappointment and frustration. As the flow ceased she slumped forward, deflated, as the final prize was snatched away. Sarah would be so good when she was trained. Everything about her, every natural instinct was to seek out pleasure.

Chang towelled her dry. His movements were almost brusque now, the coarse cotton bringing a pleasant pink glow to the girl's creamy flesh. Once she was dry he rubbed a fragrant oil into her skin. It was an oil Casswell had had specially blended for occasions such as this. The heady scent of sandalwood and ylang ylang filled the bathroom, mixing with half a dozen other exotic aromas.

Casswell's pulse quickened. He had brought the perfume back from the Far East. It was the perfume of pure desire; the perfume of pleasure and pain mixed on a palette of creamy white flesh.

The little man's hands worked rhythmically up and down the girl's slim body, highlighting the taut bands of muscle in her thighs and across her belly and breasts. It wouldn't be long now, Casswell thought, before she was ready for him.

Behind the leather mask Sarah teetered helplessly on the edge of ecstasy. It seemed no part of her was spared Chang's knowing touch. Every inch of her skin glowed. It felt as if his caresses had lulled her into a strange waking sleep; a place between worlds where she was both calm and incredibly excited.

Just as she began to think the massage would go on forever, Chang lifted her down. To her relief he held her tight, as she knew her legs would buckle. Without hesitation he picked her up in his arms as if she weighed no more than a feather. What surprised her most was the sensation of his bare flesh touching hers; she had no idea he had taken off his tunic jacket to bathe and shave her. His flesh was as smooth as alabaster and almost as cool.

Her journey in Chang's arms was not a long one. After a few minutes he once again lifted her onto what she assumed was a hook. Her feet this time rested on what felt like carpet. She moved a little to see if she could touch anything with her body, but there was nothing within reach.

Chang spread her legs, his fingers working down towards her ankles. She felt his breath on her belly and across the newly naked contours of her quim. Was it her imagination or did he breathe more deeply as he passed her sex, drinking in the oceanic perfume of her excitement?

Something snapped into place around her ankles. Sarah fought the need to cry out in panic. She was completely secured now – spread-eagled – and there was nothing she could do but wait. As the seconds ticked past every sense reached out into the darkness to find some clue as to what might follow.

Rigel Casswell stretched like a sleek big cat and then accepted the riding crop Chang offered him. It was short and flexible with a cruel bite, but was unlikely to break the skin if properly applied. Casswell stepped closer to Sarah. In the subdued light of his dressing room she seemed to be suffused with an inner glow. Her body glistened with oil, and between her breasts he could see tiny beads of perspiration. She was afraid, she was excited, and she was totally at his mercy.

He took a deep breath, drew back the head of the riding crop and laid on the first stroke. As the leather exploded against her pale flesh Sarah screamed, her breasts thrust forward, her skin seemed to grow taut with an almost dazzling brilliance. As she bucked and writhed against

41

the manacles Casswell could see the soft inner folds of her sex, and the tight puckering of her backside peeping provocatively between her rounded buttocks. He smiled and drew the crop back again…

The first stroke had caught Sarah completely by surprise. She screamed in horror and fear as the red-hot pain seared across her buttocks. The sensation spread like magma from its epicentre, making her fight against her restraints. All logical thought had left with that first stroke – all that remained was sensation. For one stunning all engulfing moment she knew she was experiencing exactly what Beatrice had felt under the cruel but impassioned hands of her lord and master.

She screamed again as the second stroke exploded across her back. The sound came from somewhere deep inside, from some dark nameless space that was purely instinctual. Here, in this ancient place, there was no holding back, no lies, no compromise, only the raw truth of pain. The pure intensity of the sensations stunned her. And now, as the crop bit home again, she understood what Beatrice meant by a desire so dark and unholy that she could give it no name.

She whimpered as the crop found its mark again, while her sex responded like a beast. Hungry and raw she could feel her need for release building deep inside. She heard the hiss of the crop as it cut through the air, and cried out again, bucking as Casswell – for she sensed it had to be him – laid on again and again and again, lifting livid weals cross her ripe flesh.

And then, just when she thought she might faint and could sense the pull of unconsciousness, she felt hands on her belly, on her arms, gently lifting her down. She collapsed against her rescuer, sobbing like a child.

Without a word, Casswell rolled her over onto her hands and knees. A hand slipped between her trembling thighs, exploring the soft wet reaches of her sex. She moaned hungrily, longing for him now to finish the deed, to make her his, to bring her to the point of no return. And still blindfolded and tied, she could do nothing to impede his explorations.

She felt his cock brush her thighs, felt his hands cup the tingling flesh of her breasts, fingers working cruelly at their sensitive peaks, rolling and nipping, and then the slow, slow progress of his cock as it pressed home into the pit of her sex.

She was wet; she knew her excitement was trickling like gossamer onto her thighs, its rich perfume mingling with the scent of Chang's massage oils. For what seemed like an eternity her virginal body fought him and held him back. He pressed forward again, this time his fingers helping to ease his curving shaft home. Still her body refused him entry. The pain of him trying to breach her maidenhood filled Sarah's mind like a red storm cloud.

'Please...' she begged on a ragged outward breath, unsure whether she was begging Casswell to stop or to carry on. Gently, he pulled her closer, murmuring soft words of encouragement, and sought again to enter that untried, untouched way. His fingers circled down over her belly to search out the bead of her clitoris – and instinctively her belly dropped lower, her pelvis tipping to allow him deeper.

She blushed furiously under her mask as she realised how hungrily her body demanded him. It was pure animal desire that was guiding her now. Her muscles flexed again, wanting him in her, encouraging him deeper. She felt like a bitch on heat, whining and fretting on the end of a leash, anxious only to be covered. Casswell pressed down on her pleasure bud and then thrust forward again. Sarah shrieked with a mixture of pain and pleasure as he finally breached her, tears forming in her eyes behind the leather mask.

She was truly his now, there was no way of undoing what had been done. Casswell gripped her hips and pulled her closer still, stroking her belly and her breasts, his muscular thighs beating a rhythm against hers.

She sensed his pleasure and delight in her body. It was a striking contrast to the brutality of the beating, but then again, what had Casswell left to prove?

Hadn't she already agreed to stay at the house and give herself willingly to him? No amount of cruelty or kindness on his part would undo that simple act of submission. He plunged deeper, and his fingers locked in her hair as he jerked her up, her body tensed into an erotic arc against his. Instinct told her he was almost at the point of no return, and the knowledge electrified her.

She gasped, hearing his breath roar in her ears and feeling those terrifying thrusts become less and less refined. Her own excitement could not be held in check for much longer. Despite the rawness between her legs her body bayed for release. The merest brush of Casswell's thumb over the engorged ridge of her clitoris was enough to complete the cycle of pleasure.

Sarah cried out as she began to lose control. Her newly breached sex contracted like a silken fist, drawing Casswell yet deeper inside. Low in her belly a glittering crystal spiral of pleasure seemed to pulse like a beacon with every contraction, filling her whole body with white light. She sobbed as the waves of orgasm crashed through them both.

Crouched above her, Casswell shuddered, thrusting forward to milk the zenith of his pleasure, stabbing deeper and deeper, helpless to resist the call of his desire.

As the lights finally exploded in her head, he pushed deeper still and Sarah screamed his name, her whole being controlled by instincts that were older than time itself. The sensations seemed to go on and on – until, at long last, there was only stillness and quiet.

Chapter Four

That night Sarah dreamt of Beatrice de Fleur. In her imagination the two young women stood either side of a mirror, divided not by desire, but by time. In the dream Sarah reached out to touch her kindred spirit only to have her vanish, leaving Doctor Rigel Casswell standing in her place. Or was it Casswell? Perhaps it was Beatrice's dark lord, the man with eyes like a hawk, a whip cradled in his hand. In her dream, Sarah stepped through the mirror into his waiting arms, naked and powerless to resist him.

When Sarah woke up she was cold, and for an instant had no idea where she was. It was still dark. As she tried to focus her thoughts images from Beatrice's journal floated back into her mind. The girl's words filled her head and, like misty wraiths, formed memories of intense sensations, mixing in turn with the images from her dreams.

And then Sarah remembered exactly where she was...

Despite the darkness she blushed crimson. The things she remembered were not just from Beatrice's diary. As she tried to turn over her arms and back screamed in protest. Everything was coming back to her in vivid detail.

She was at Casswell Hall, tied to the bed in the guest room. Still manacled, she had been secured by a length of chain to the head of the bed. The blindfold had been removed, and she could just about make out the interior of the room in the glow from the hearth.

She had been secured with enough chain to allow her to sit up, and she winced as the movements reminded her of the kiss of the Doctor's whip. Even in the gloom her skin still gleamed with the remains of the fragrant oil. Bedclothes lay rumpled on the floor beside the bed...

Sarah froze. She was not alone. She could just detect someone breathing, and knew then that the bedding had not slipped from her, but had been lifted away.

A shadow suddenly moved. Hands grabbed her ankles and jerked her sharply down the bed, pulling the chain and her arms taut. Sarah shrieked as the unseen hands secured her ankles to the foot of the bed. She pulled furiously against the restraints.

'Who's there?' she called into the gloom, her voice shrill with trepidation. 'Who is it?!'

The hands stroked up her calves. She stretched, peering into the darkness, trying to see her tormentor. She saw the shadow. It was squat, and Sarah knew it was Chang. Chang, who had seemed unmoved by her preparations for Casswell. Chang, who had hidden his own desires so well and waited patiently until his master's passion was spent.

She had no idea what to expect from the little Oriental, and tensed as his finger stroked across the outer lips of her sex, damp still from Casswell's attentions. Slipping one hand under her buttocks he lifted her body up towards him. She felt rather than saw him lower his head and sniff her. She blushed furiously, imaging the perfume that must fill his nostrils – a scent of desire and Casswell's seed – and then slowly he moved closer. His breath moved across the exposed rise of her quim, and then he parted her lips with his tongue.

She gasped as the very tip found her clitoris and lapped at its sensitive hood. His delicate touch electrified her, his caress creating an intense, almost painful ripple of pleasure. She was astonished by the sensations his mouth evoked. Fingers joined the tongue, dipping into the moist pit between her legs, spreading her juice out over her thighs.

Sarah was astonished; his touch was as light as a breath, and yet she could already feel her excitement building. His fingers slipped lower, caressing the sensitive bridge of flesh between the tight depths of her quim and the forbidden closure behind. A finger circled the puckered ring of her anus and Sarah stiffened. Although the sensation was far from unpleasant, she suddenly understood what his true goal was.

His tongue renewed its delicate ballet around her clitoris, one hand rising momentarily to stroke her throbbing nipples with the juice that trickled from between her legs. But Sarah was aware now of what Chang really had in mind. Everything else he was doing was a distraction, a sleight of hand to make her relax and forget his true intentions. His fingers worked their magic, stroking lubrication over the tight rosebud to smooth his course.

She tensed, afraid now, as he sought entry while his tongue spun on and on, a magic caress that was fast propelling part of her consciousness towards oblivion.

As the pleasure began to escalate he pressed a finger inside that dark passageway and she cried out in confusion. At first her body refused him – and then he breached her. The sense of tightness in the forbidden closure took her breath away. Still he gently but firmly pressed deeper. She cried out again; embarrassed and afraid – while her rogue body drew him deeper still.

Chang's face lifted, leaving a single finger buried deep in each of her most secret places. His expression was unreadable in the shadows but his eyes glittered like fire.

'Why don't you relax and come with me?' he whispered, his voice so low that at first she wondered if she'd imagined it. 'There is nothing you can do to resist.'

'I – I'll t-tell Doctor Casswell…' she stammered weakly, struggling to find her voice. 'D-does he know about this?'

Chang snorted. 'Oh Sarah. This isn't like school. There's no point telling tales. He will say nothing because you will say nothing. While you are staying here at the hall your welfare depends on me. It would be better to learn compliance and smooth your path.'

Sarah stared up at him. As their eyes met through the darkness his thumb brushed her clitoris, sending a flare of pleasure spiralling through her belly. She groaned, her body flexing up to him, lifting on the wings of instinct. Her sex closed around his finger and she realised with horror that the contraction was echoed deep in her backside too.

Chang grinned at her obvious discomfort. 'A little too tight for me yet, lady,' he said as his fingers slithered from her body.

Sarah sighed with relief, but it was short-lived. A bedside lamp flicked on. The sudden glare made her wince and turn her head away, but he clearly didn't care about her discomfort. With deceptive strength he rolled her onto her side so she was facing away from him.

'But that can be easily remedied,' he continued.

'What are you doing to me?' she whimpered.

The silence that followed made her shiver. Whatever

he had in mind she could offer no resistance.

'Chang, please—' but before she could finish her plea she felt his hands part her sore buttocks, and knowing fingers seeking the forbidden entry they had so recently vacated.

Sarah flushed scarlet and began to protest again.

Chang leant over her. 'Better too if you learn when silence is most appropriate.' He cupped her full breasts, stroking the swollen buds as if to comfort her. 'Take a deep breath and pant, this will stretch you.' His caress was almost hypnotic, and then she felt something nosing at the puckered rosebud of her backside.

Her body closed tight and she squealed anxiously, panting as he had suggested, willing her body not to resist the slow unrelenting progress of the oiled dildo that slid into her anus. Her humiliation seemed complete as Chang's hands worked between her thighs, strapping a belt on that would hold the little stretcher in position.

As he worked his fingers dipped into her quim. Despite the cocktail of shame and trepidation her sex closed hungrily around them. Sarah was mortified. Her body demanded his touch, even if her mind rejected it. She could feel him stroking the dildo through the thin muscular membrane that divided her sex from the passageway behind. Sarah held every muscle taut, the sensation of fullness and tension terrifying her.

Seemingly satisfied, he grunted and pulled away. His hands linked around her belly, and to her surprise he turned her again, onto her front and then up onto her knees. Her face was buried in the bedclothes, and her buttocks were thrust high and stretched around the intrusive tube of plastic.

His fingers dipped into her sex, casually brushing her

clitoris and rekindling her pleasure. It was sweet torture, the intensity heightened by the sleek contours of the stretcher buried deep in her bottom. She shivered, knowing that at some time Chang or his master fully intended to replace that plastic with the real thing.

Chang stalked around the bed, checking the security of her bondage. He then stooped, kissed her tensed buttocks in turn, and eased her down until she lay flat on the soft bed.

'I will see you in the morning,' he whispered into her ear. 'Sleep now.'

Sarah cried out in frustration, her body almost at the point of release.

'Come back,' she begged, astonished that she could want him after what he had done to her. 'Please don't leave me like this. Please, Chang… I need you…' But her words were wasted. If he was there he didn't respond, though she knew in her heart he had already gone.

Sarah closed her eyes, a single tear soaking into the tumble of sheets which cocooned her flushed face. Her whole body was taut, and between her legs still glowed the unfulfilled ache for pleasure that Chang had ignited, but not extinguished.

From behind the unblinking eye of the mirror Doctor Casswell peered into the gloom with a growing sense of delight; Chang had completed the next stage of Sarah's preparation.

Chapter Five

...Today, when the afternoon shadows had begun to lengthen and I and the children's nurse were sitting together in the long gallery, my lord sent for me. To my great relief he did not send that blaggard, Arturo, but a new pageboy called Michael, who serves at my lady's table. The boy begged that I hurry and follow him, and I did as I was bidden.

My master waited a little distance from the castle, in the old walled garden down beside the river. My heart quickened with desire as I saw him standing there amongst the trees, although I blushed as our eyes met, ashamed to feel so brazen, so wanton, but even so I hurried across the grass towards him...

It was nine o'clock the following morning and Chang had just cleared away Sarah's breakfast things. And it seemed as if she was expected to carry on with her work as if nothing at all had happened.

If only that were possible.

She had been woken early by the little Oriental man, who had removed the anal stretcher and then untied her as if such behaviour was an everyday occurrence. He had then announced that breakfast would be served in the study at eight and left as if nothing had happened between them. He behaved as if the events of the night were normal.

Although she had showered Sarah still felt unclean,

and deep inside she could still feel the ghost of the stretcher. Memories of the night filled her mind; the passion and pain and humiliation. She tried to focus her attention on the neat lines of handwritten text. She knew that if only she could concentrate for a line or two she would be drawn into Beatrice's compelling narrative. She switched on the computer and turned her attentions back to Doctor Casswell's transcript of Beatrice's manuscript:

...I could sense a brooding hunger that excited me beyond all measure, and see that my lord's eyes were dark with desire. And I knew I wanted nothing more at that moment than to do as he bade me, whatever it might be; my body was his alone to command. My sex moistened at the thought of his touch, his lips, his kisses, the cruel bite of his whip on my flesh as I writhed, bound and helpless, waiting for his pleasure.

By all the saints, such demons, such devilry, such desire has filled my thoughts and my dreams since he took me that day in his apartments, I cannot tell you. Even my humiliation at the hands of Arturo and the priest Orme has done nothing to stem the flow of fire that bubbles in my veins. I cannot help but wonder if I will ever be safe from these thoughts.

'You are late, girl. What kept you?' he snapped.

I began to protest and only then realised that he was not alone. Until that moment I had not seen that deep in the shadows stood both Father Orme and another, unknown, noble man who watched my approach with equal interest.

'Lift you dress, wench,' the noble man ordered. I slowed my step and hesitated for an instant.

'Do as the Lord Usher says,' says my master and, seeing the look of approval and encouragement on my master's face, I did exactly as I was told. But even as I lifted my heavy skirts Lord Usher's expression hardened.

'What folly is this?' he growled furiously, indicating my undergarments.

My lord turned to me. 'Take them off, Beatrice. I would have you naked under your robes, girl, from now on. No more of these pantaloons and petticoats. Take them off. Have I not explained to you, you are mine? Mine as and when I command, not held at bay by linen and wool. Take them off!'

I blushed, eyes downcast, and nodded. I understood that he meant for me to be always at his beck and call, always ready to be touched by him and others if he so chose. I slipped off my petticoats. He nodded his approval and then indicated that I should hold my robes all the higher so that his compatriots might examine my nakedness.

The stranger stepped a little closer and ran a hand over my belly, and then down through the dark curls that frame my sex.

'Would you have me undo her bodice for you, Cousin?' asked my lord. 'A finer a pair of sweet tits you'll have trouble to find this side of the city.'

The man snorted and shook his head. 'Nay, here in my hand I have the only thing that truly interests me.' His fingers tightened on my quim. 'I would wish that our maker had had the good sense to strike the whole of the female sex deaf and dumb so that I could fuck them all without having to worry about talking to them or wooing them or other such pointless posturing.' He grinned. 'And there'd be no risk of them telling tales to their men folk or their fathers.' He nodded towards Father Orme. 'What say you?'

Orme shrugged, apparently unoffended by the man's blasphemy.

Lord Usher's fingers had already found their way between the lips of my quim into that most intimate of places. I looked frantically at my master, praying he might rescue me from this brutal stranger, but he ignored my shame and humiliation and coolly watched the nobleman explore me.

Usher plunged his finger home now, making me wince at his roughness. He grinned at my discomfort, his thumb lifting to trace the rise of my pleasure bud. In spite of myself, my body responded to his rough caress, and I shivered.

The man laughed triumphantly. 'See, there you have it, my lord, deprived of the right to answer back all women are the same. The little vixen wants nothing more than to feel my cock buried to the hilt inside her. Can you not see it in her eyes and the way she moves against me? Away with all this courtly love and poetry, give me the honest lust of a tight cunt and a fine wet mouth any day. Unless of course you are too old or too tired to care, don't waste conversation on harlots such as this. It is here and only here that the real pleasure lies.' As he spoke he spread the traitorous juices from my sex out onto my thighs and belly.

He addressed only my master and Orme, without a word for me or a thought for the shame and distress I might feel at his words or his cruel invasion of my body. I understand now that he saw me not as a person but as a being below contempt, a thing to be used, reduced to nothing more than the essence of my sex.

Lifting his fingers, he drew one of them into his mouth and smacked his lips as if the traces of juice it bore were the finest of delicacies. Pulling me closer he unfastened his robe, and without prelude pushed my legs wide apart and guided his cock into me, pulling one leg up around his waist to give him better purchase. The moment of coupling was so quick, so unexpected, that I cried out in horror and surprise.

He grinned as he plunged his engorged member home. 'I like it when a woman calls out as you enter her. 'Tis an honest animal cry of desire and need.'

I shivered as he forced himself deeper, closing his eyes with the sheer pleasure of my body closing around him.

'Just as you said, dear Cousin, she is good and tight,' he murmured thickly to my master and then, to my surprise, after no more than a dozen strokes, pulled his cock out. Its livid purple crown brushed across my thighs like a wet quarterstaff.

He grinned as I looked up at him, and then he forced me roughly down onto my hands and knees. I knew what he expected. Without even looking at me he guided his shaft between my lips and into my mouth.

I shuddered as the taste of my own excitement invaded my senses. My sex fluttered like a bird's wing, and without thinking where I was or what I was doing, I slid a hand down over my belly, scrabbling up the hem of my gown to find to the soft wet places that dwelt beneath. To my horror the stranger laughed, even as my tongue and free hand worked furiously along his great shaft.

'By all the saints, it is true what they say about country wenches. Come and mount up, Orme. Or perhaps you, good Cousin. Come, make some use of this girl and share the pleasures her untutored passions offer. By God, she is hot!'

Glancing to one side, I saw the lecherous expression on Orme's face. 'Unfasten your bodice, wench,' he said, in a throaty tone that betrayed his excitement. 'I would play a little with those shapely dugs that the good Lord Usher dismisses as the province of babes. If you have no objection, my lord?' He glanced in my master's direction.

My master waved them on, and by doing so commanded me to do as I was told. I could see the desire in his eyes, and tell from his expression that when his friends were done with me he had a plan of his own.

While I loosened the fastenings of my bodice Orme knelt behind me and his cold talons clawed up my skirts. He raked his nails across my flesh as he guided his shaft into my quim.

Leaning forward, he jerked down the shoulders of my petticoats, and those same talons caught hold of my freed breasts. Cupping their delicate flesh he began to nip and twist at their swollen buds. His stale, rasping breath quickened as I cried out in pain. But my pain delighted him, and I felt a dark mixture of shame and heat rising from deep inside me. Upon my lips I could taste the growing pleasure of Lord Usher. I knew it wouldn't be long before his seed filled my mouth, and I prayed, as my own body began to respond to their growing excitement, that God might save me from this divine torment...

Sarah shivered, responding instinctively to the account of Beatrice's intense emotions. Her own feelings simmered. She took a deep breath, unable to comprehend what was happening to her; as she transferred Beatrice's story onto the computer screen it felt as if every nuance, every sensation, was echoed in her own body.

Was this what Casswell had hoped for, so her initiation into this world of pain and pleasure might be all the smoother? Sarah closed her eyes, and at once her mind was awash with a heady mix of images from the night before and from Beatrice's diary.

Out beyond the windows of the study, Sarah could see a crumbling terrace and the gentle rise and fall of the overgrown gardens as they tumbled down over a low incline towards dense woodland. She tried to concentrate on their rich greenery; fighting to calm her mind. Once, the gardens must have been magnificent.

She picked up the file and turned to the next page. It seemed that the boundaries between the past and the present had already begun to blur.

Chapter Six

...Finally, when Lord Usher and Father Orme had done with me, my master approached. I was crouched on the rough grass on all fours, breasts and backside bare, with the taste of Usher's seed still on my lips and tongue, and the old priest's pleasure trickling down the insides of my thighs.

I could feel the colour rushing to my cheeks, imagining the picture I presented to my lord, huddled there under the canopy of trees like some wild forest spirit, a creature of passion, reduced to the very essence of being.

My lord's eyes were dark with unspent desire. He circled me while Lord Usher adjusted his clothing.

''Tis a fine prize you have there,' Usher said to my master. 'When you are weary of her, perhaps you will consider a trade.'

But his voice seemed no more than a bird call on the wind, as distant as the sound of the tide upon a foreign shore, for as our eyes met there seemed to be just the two of us; only I and my lord caught together by this dark alchemy. Nothing Orme or the Lord Usher can ever do to me will match the passion I feel for my master.

He caught hold of my hair and jerked me up. As our lips met I felt my heart soar and my stomach flutter. It makes no sense; what spell is this, what unholy magic is it that binds me so tight to him, this man who humiliates me and having stole my virtue brings me into such debauchery?

He kissed me hard, his tongue driving deep into my mouth as if to seek out the seed of his compatriot, and then he dropped me back onto the grass, and slipped off his belt. My pulse raced as I watched him wind the buckled end around his fist, leaving the other hanging like a livid tongue. And as he did he asked who I considered to be my master. Is this some game, some ritual to entrap me?

I answered him as before. 'Why you, sir. You know I am pledged to serve you and your family.'

And then he laughed, momentarily easing the tension between us. 'I had thought, Beatrice, that your powers would be diluted once you were broken, but it seems I have underestimated you. What a prize you are, sweet little Beatrice. I am to be your master in all things. Your body, your very soul belongs to me now. Do you understand?'

I nodded. How well I understood.

His voice lowered a little and the humour left his eyes; desire returning like the moon's rise. 'I will teach you how a maid should truly serve her master.'

I knew I had heard these words before. These were the things he had said in his chamber. But before I could reply the broad leather belt exploded across my rump. I screamed out in pain and surprise as the raw fire spread out like a molten veil across my flesh.

'Trust me, Beatrice, trust me and give yourself to me completely,' he murmured breathlessly as the next stroke found its mark. 'So brazen – so ripe. I already know you are mine to command. Give yourself to me and I will not betray your trust. I will show you paradise. You are mine now, do you understand?'

'Yes, yes,' I sobbed, as the belt cracked out again.

What did he want me to say? Through the haze of pain I wondered whether Usher and Orme had stayed to watch this final act – or once their own passions were spent had their interest waned?

The belt found its mark again and again, and with each stroke I screamed. Even now my body glows white-hot with the memory of that cruel unspeakable hunger, which the kiss of the leather both fed and created.

By all the saints I craved to feel him against me then, buried to the hilt in my quim, which craved the sweet release of a climax. And as my body reached out for that pinnacle my master dropped the belt and threw me to the ground.

Gathering up my ragged skirt, he lifted my hips and drove his cock deep inside me. The ferocity of his entry took my breath away. He gripped my shoulders and pulled me up, so that I knelt astride him, and while his fingers clawed at my raw back he drove deeper still.

My naked breasts pressed tight against the cold leather of his waistcoat, my nipples brushing against the studded metal emblems of his house.

It seems no more than an instant before we both reached that ancient ground where all reason is lost and all that remains is pure pleasure. I cried out with delight as the first waves shuddered through me; waves of fire, waves of ice – while deep inside I could feel my lord's erupting pleasure echoing my own.

And then, just as my lord pulled away, I saw someone hiding amongst the trees. Not Orme. Not Usher. It was another, and my heart leapt with terror as I recognised the spy...

'Miss Morgan?'

Sarah jumped as if she'd been shot. In the doorway Doctor Casswell was watching her with interest. She blushed, wondering how long he had been standing there. Hastily she closed Beatrice's journal, but before she could speak, he said, 'I thought perhaps you would care to join me for lunch today?'

Sarah struggled to find her voice. 'That... that would be lovely.'

Casswell nodded and extended a hand in invitation. As she got to her feet he waved the hand a little higher. 'Lift your skirt, Miss Morgan.'

Sarah stared at him in astonishment. Between her legs she could still feel the flurries of pleasure that Beatrice's words had already ignited; she knew her body was hungry for satisfaction. She looked up at Casswell almost defiantly. Who did he think he was? Did he think she wouldn't dare behave so brazenly? She held the hem of her skirt and lifted it to her waist, her eyes meeting his in an unspoken challenge.

Casswell sighed and shook his head. 'It seems that, like Beatrice, you do not understand what is expected of you, Sarah. While you are here at Casswell Hall you will be available as and when I require it. Take those off,' he indicated her knickers and tights. 'From now on you will be naked under your outer garments at all times, though I have no objection to stockings and a suspender belt. I will have Chang arrange it for you. Come closer.'

Sarah was still struggling to take off her tights and panties, but she did as he said. Standing in front of him, her body pale and exposed in the bright sunlight from the window, she shivered as he stared down at her. His examination was perfunctory; no more than a glance at her naked sex and the gentle swell of her belly. She dropped the hem of her skirt and waited.

She knew this was some kind of test. He was making her wait for whatever was to follow; making her understand that he was in charge – not her.

The seconds ticked by.

All she could hear clearly was the excited beat of her heart pulsing in her ears. She looked up, and for an instant she saw her need reflected in Casswell's dark pupils.

He indicated that she should lift her skirt again, and she did so without a second thought, trembling as he slipped a hand between her legs and cupped her shaven quim. A single finger traced the moist outer lips. His eyes darkened and he nodded his approval.

'Good. I want you to understand that this is how you will remain during your stay here. Now, remove your bra.'

Sarah stepped away from him, wondering what on earth she was doing as her trembling fingers fumbled clumsily with each button of her blouse. The white cotton was so sheer that she knew once her bra was removed her nipples, as dark and hard as cherries, would peek through for anyone to see.

She slowed her pace; perhaps there was a way she could soften Casswell's demeanour. She turned a little, and flirtatiously slipped the blouse back off her shoulders, posing so that Casswell would get a good view of her full ripe breasts.

To her horror Casswell snorted derisively. 'Oh please, do not flirt with me, Miss Morgan. I already have what I want from you, there really is no need to try and ensnare me. Now hurry and do as I say.'

Humiliated and blushing furiously, Sarah did as she

was told.

When she had removed her bra and replaced her blouse, Casswell asked, 'Does reading about Beatrice excite you?'

She wondered that he needed to ask. 'Yes,' she murmured thickly.

How could she explain it was the most electrifying thing she had ever read? He nodded and then, opening a drawer in his desk, removed something that looked like a small oar. Made from leather it was as broad as a human hand with a short flexible handle. Sarah stared at it, and then at him.

'What's that for?' she whispered, though she had already guessed.

Casswell's expression hardened. 'You will learn not to be so curious or so quick to speak. Bend over the desk. You need to be punished.'

Sarah gasped. 'Punished? But what have I done?'

Casswell sighed. 'It's a question of attitude, Sarah. Your ridiculous attempt at flirtation is a case in point.' He indicated the bundle of underwear she held in her hands. 'And those—'

'But I didn't know—' Sarah began, but the doctor's face was impassive. It seemed ignorance of the house rules was no defence. He indicated the desk. She slowly backed up until her buttocks rested on the very edge of the polished mahogany.

Casswell's expression and tone hardened. 'Please, Miss Morgan, don't toy with me. Turn around and lift up your skirt!'

Sarah shivered. Although his voice was not raised there was an authoritative edge to it that was impossible to ignore. She did as he commanded, and then waited anxiously while he examined his prize.

When the blow came the severity took her breath away. The leather paddle hit her low on the buttocks, making her shriek with pain. The sensation was more diffused than the crop. From the corner of her eye she caught sight of Casswell an instant before he hit her again. He was a man entranced, caught up in the strange enchantment that Beatrice had so eloquently described.

'A dozen, I think,' he murmured, as the paddle found its mark again.

Sarah slumped forward, supporting her weight on her forearms, while between her legs the growing mixture of pleasure and pain was almost more than she could bear.

Casswell smiled as the paddle exploded across Sarah's pink flesh. Leaning over the desk, breathing hard, with her skirt gathered up around her waist, she was a compelling sight. Her buttocks were rounded and full, a delightful contrast to her narrow waist. Both orbs glowed, the livid blush cut here and there by the kiss of the crop from the night before. Between the curves, as she struggled to regain her composure, he could see tantalising glimpses of her sex; plump, ripe, and ready. It would be easy to move closer, slide a hand between those firm thighs and bring her to the climax her body demanded and she so richly deserved. And yet he denied her, and himself, that release.

He dropped the paddle to the floor and ordered her to stand and turn around. She looked contrite, but the downcast eyes and flushed cheeks did nothing to fool him. She could not disguise the way her nipples jutted forward through the thin fabric of her blouse, dark and ripe as rosebuds, any more than she had been able to disguise the wet folds of her quim, glistening with excitement as she had writhed and twisted away from the paddle. Sarah Morgan was such a find, such a treasure.

Casswell beckoned her a little closer and idly traced one of her nipples through the sheer blouse. She rewarded him with the softest of moans. Her eyes closed and her moist lips peeled apart. Beneath his fingertips he could feel her trembling.

'Have you a jacket?' he asked quietly.

She nodded.

'Go and fetch it, and I'll ask Chang to find you some stockings. We'll be eating at the Boar's Head, in Brenwell.'

Sarah opened her eyes and looked at him. 'We're eating out?'

Casswell nodded, choosing to ignore the surprise in her tone.

'Sarah,' he said in a voice that allowed for no contradictions. 'I expect to be obeyed without question and, from now on, I expect you to remain silent unless spoken to.' He waved her away, aware of the flash of indignation in the young woman's eyes. 'Don't be long,' he added as she moved unsteadily for the door.

Ten minutes later Sarah was seated in the car beside him, and they were heading down a narrow country lane towards a hamlet that nestled in the wooded valley below Casswell Hall.

As they rounded a bend on an isolated stretch of road, Casswell spotted two rough-looking lads hitchhiking towards town. As he passed them he slowed the car. The youths – perhaps in their late teens or early twenties – looked up as Casswell's Bentley purred past, and then began to hurry toward him as he applied the brakes and eased the car into reverse.

'Lift your skirt a little higher, my dear,' he said, laying his arm across the back of her seat and looking over his shoulder to manoeuvre the car back up the lane.

Sarah looked at him in astonishment, and was about to say something when she caught the look on his face.

'Now,' he said more firmly. Momentarily he saw another flash of rebellion in her eyes, and then the same hunger he'd seen earlier. It was a heady combination; her spirit delighted him. As they glided back towards the running youths, she did as he said, sliding the skirt up her stockinged thighs until it barely covered her sex. Casswell smiled thinly. 'Good, now take off your jacket too. After all, we are expecting company.'

Sarah stared at him, and then back at the boys. 'What – what do expect from me? I won't—'

Casswell's expression hardened, his amusement at her behaviour and her insolence rapidly wearing thin. 'You will learn to obey me, Sarah,' he cut her off. 'One way or the other, you will learn. The punishment you received this morning was nothing compared to what can happen.'

The car stopped silently and one of the rough young men bobbed down to glance in the passenger window. Sarah's jacket, though not yet removed, was undone far enough to reveal the ripe curve of her breasts beneath the thin cotton shirt. The youth drank in the tableau and grinned salaciously before wiping his lips with the back of his hand.

Casswell lowered the electric window. 'An interesting view, wouldn't you say?'

The hiker laughed nervously, clearly not quite sure if Casswell meant what he thought. 'Going anywhere near

Castlemead, are you?' He spoke with a strong country accent, and despite addressing the urbane driver, his eyes hungrily roamed over Sarah's long legs, the sheer black silk stockings, the suspenders, and the promise of what lay beyond the raised hem of her neatly tailored skirt.

Casswell raised his hands in apology. 'Sadly, Castlemead isn't on our way. But perhaps we might be able to come to some sort of mutually beneficial arrangement?'

Now joined by his companion, the leering youth continued to stare into the car while waiting to hear what Casswell might have to offer. Sarah blushed furiously.

Casswell smiled at her discomfort. He could see a hint perspiration dampening her brow and fringe, while the male youths' lust was as raw and undisguised as if they were in rut. He nodded toward Sarah. 'My young friend here is new to this area. Perhaps you boys might like to take her for a little walk and show her some of the sights? I'm sure she would like to take in a little local colour.'

The more brazen of the two was a thickset lout with stubble on his chin. He grinned cautiously at Casswell's suggestion, and then pulled up his sleeves as if to bring a certain business-like quality to the proceedings. His forearms were a mass of swirling multi-coloured tattoos that promised everything from constant fidelity to sudden death.

'And why would we want to do that?' he asked carefully.

'Why not?'

The youth visibly relaxed a little, and Casswell knew the simplicity of his answer had done the trick.

'Yeah... why not,' he grinned widely and licked his lips with a fat tongue. 'After all, it's a nice day for a walk. Maybe you might like to come along and keep her company – you know, keep an eye on us? You know… watch…?' he said, imbuing the words with all the erotic possibilities he could muster. 'Is that what you're into?' His gaze flitted from Sarah's thighs to Casswell, and quickly back again.

Casswell nodded.

What a perceptive youth. His eyes told of something that Casswell instinctively recognised as animal cunning. In fact, his whole demeanour gave the impression that he was something barely tame; a feral creature that might turn at any second. It added a certain frisson to the encounter that appealed to Casswell.

'Perhaps that might be a good idea,' he said, and as he spoke he pulled a twenty-pound note from his wallet, and leaning across Sarah he handed it to the wild youth. 'And here's something for your trouble.'

The youth acknowledged its receipt with the slightest nod of his head.

'And when we've had our little walk,' Casswell continued, 'we'll give you both a lift down to the village. We just need to get off the main road now.'

The two stepped away from the car, and Casswell smiled at the ashen Sarah as he pulled the purring vehicle into a nearby lay-by cut into the verge.

Sarah's seduction was a joy to watch. The two youths led her into a ramshackle barn a few hundred yards away from the lane, and there they took her with such vigour and faultless timing that Casswell wondered with amusement if they spent their young lives sharing women. Perhaps they did. Perhaps the more brash of the two, the tattooed negotiator, brought the prey down in the chase, and then carried them back to their lair where the younger could share the spoils of the hunt.

Perhaps the most erotic episode of the encounter was when the quieter of the two tied Sarah to a rusting ring set in one wall. She didn't fight him. Although she whimpered pitifully as the rope tightened, he had no trouble in securing an old length of rope around her wrists and then through the ring.

She was a picture of submissive beauty; the repressed little secretary totally undone by such an outlandish encounter. She looked superb with her clothing and hair dishevelled, and her arms stretched and secured above her head.

Casswell could see a rivulet of perspiration trickling down between her breasts. She was intensely excited! Oh, that much was so obvious! And she trembled like a timid kitten as the unlikely pair moved in to bring the game to its heady conclusion.

Sarah had not spoken throughout the episode. There was a glazed expression in her eyes as if she was caught up in a dream, and Casswell knew, despite her revulsion, that the dark desire within was being fed by the two unschooled ruffians.

To Casswell's delight, as soon as she was secured against the wall, the quieter one dropped to his knees amongst the straw and began to nuzzle feverishly between her quivering thighs. Finding the riches that dripped like honey from her gaping sex, he lapped at her hungrily. Sarah slumped on the end of the old rope and whimpered her delight and shame as the youth found the bud that throbbed there. He held her open with nicotine-stained fingers, and Casswell could hear his active tongue slurping against her as she shuddered wearily towards the orgasm she so clearly craved.

Her lashes fluttered, and she peered down with glazed eyes at her final and total humiliation; the older of the two knelt and slipped his own revived erection between his mate's buttocks, and he buggered him most soundly.

Chapter Seven

With her jacket clutched tightly around her shoulders, Sarah hurried into the ladies' room at the Boar's Head Hotel and slammed the door behind her. The elegant little powder room, tucked away under the main staircase, was quietly luxurious; decorated in pastel pinks and creams with a row of gold, harp-backed chairs neatly arranged under the grey marble vanity unit. It was a world away from the wild events in the barn.

An elderly attendant was arranging thick cream towels over a rail. She looked up at Sarah's arrival and nodded to acknowledge her presence, but she didn't speak.

Casswell had dropped the two youths just outside the village, with more than enough money to pay for a taxi to their destination. Sarah wondered if the louts might have been tempted to follow the car; would they not want to find out more about her and Casswell; eager for a little more carnal pleasure? When she closed her eyes she could still see their eyes, as dark and beady as rats' in the fetid gloom.

She could hardly believe what she'd done, and struggled to regain some semblance of composure, forcing herself to breathe more slowly. How quiet the unruffled, perfumed surroundings of the powder room were; a stunning contrast to the shadowy intimacy of the barn where she had been just minutes earlier.

Sarah leant heavily against the vanity unit and stared at her reflection in the mirror above the basins. Was there some chance she was dreaming after all? Would she close her eyes again and wake up back at home at her aunt's house, or even in her room at Casswell Hall? The erotic images from Beatrice's diary seemed to have effected every part of her life, why not her dreams?

But Sarah knew this was no dream. A tiny flame of knowledge burned deep in her pupils, a little flare that she doubted anyone else would ever notice. Rigel Casswell had helped unleash a part of her nature she had never even suspected existed; a part that was set to change her life forever.

She opened her handbag and, as she took out her hairbrush, noticed her hands were trembling. Although her hair was still in need of a groom and her cheeks had a healthy glow about them, there was very little other outward evidence to suggest the encounter with the two anonymous young men had ever occurred.

She filled a basin with warm water and washed her face, wondering if there was any way she could wash the rest of her body. Doctor Casswell was expecting her to join him for lunch, and it wouldn't do to keep him waiting too long, but she longed to rid herself of the raw animal scent of the barn.

Sarah realised the elderly attendant was staring at her. She reddened under the old woman's unfaltering gaze, and reapplied her make up and tidied her hair.

'Is there something you want, dearie?' the woman asked when Sarah had done, looking her up and down. 'Something you need?'

'No, not really,' said Sarah, adding a final touch of lipstick, her eyes fixed on the other woman's in the mirror. 'I was just wondering if there was somewhere I could have a shower, or even just have a proper wash.'

The woman grinned, revealing a mismatch of teeth. 'I could find you somewhere nice and private if you want. You've been up to it, ain't ya?' she said with an obscene leer. 'Have you finished for today, or are you getting yourself ready to turn another trick?'

Sarah blushed furiously. 'I *beg* your pardon?' she protested indignantly. 'I'm here having lunch with someone.'

The woman grinned. 'No need to play so prim and proper with me, dearie. I know a whore when I see one. Did your client send you in here to clean yourself up?'

Utterly speechless, Sarah stared at the woman with growing incredulity.

'Or is that how he likes you best?' the hag continued, moving closer. 'Sitting beside him in full view of everyone out there, and then when you're eating maybe he'll slip a finger up you – when he thinks no one's looking.' She cackled to herself. 'Or maybe he prefers it when they are looking—'

Sarah hastily sidestepped her and started backing towards the washroom door. 'I don't know what you're talking about,' she said weakly.

'Oh really?' the old woman sneered. 'There's no need to run away from me, my lamb. I've been there. I used to be a working girl myself. I certainly don't mean you any harm. I've worked the hotels all my life. Seen it all, me. If you like I could lock the door so you can get yourself cleaned up.' She pulled a key out of her overall pocket. 'And if you're short of a pound or two there's a couple of guests staying at the moment who'd pay real well to watch you tidy yourself up. Maybe I could soap you down—' She mimed the action of cradling a heavy breast with one claw-like hand.

Sarah had to get away from the insane woman. Her fingers were on the door handle, and as the hag shuffled closer Sarah pulled it open and hastily slipped out into the busy foyer, her heart pounding in her chest.

She began to tremble, and tried to relax now that there were other people around. Had stepping into Casswell's debauched world launched her into a way of life from which there was no escape? What was it that the old woman had seen in her face that had told her so much? Sarah swallowed hard, tears forming in her eyes. She wondered if there was any way she could tell Doctor Casswell about her bizarre encounter.

The hotel was busy. The doctor was waiting for her in the bar and looked up at her arrival, a smile of approval on his face. His expression remained consistent as Sarah approached, and she felt a strange flurry of affection and desire that puzzled her. He handed her a glass of wine and indicated the stool beside him.

'You look wonderful,' he complimented as she positioned herself elegantly beside him. He lowered his voice conspiratorially, 'And you performed exceptionally well with our young friends earlier.' Sarah blushed yet again and glanced anxiously around to see if anybody was within hearing distance. Leaning a little closer, he slid a hand onto her stockinged thigh and eased her legs a little apart, his eyes firmly fixed on hers.

She understood his mute command and relaxed her legs, opening for him, submitting to the path of his exploration. The confident smile of approval widened. The brazen hand inched higher. One long finger grazed the plump lips of her sex.

He kissed her cheek lightly and whispered in her ear, 'Don't worry, no one can see what I'm doing.' As he opened her wider still, Sarah struggled to retain some shred of composure, but found it almost impossible. She sipped the glass of wine while he casually ordered lunch, the barman clearly unaware that the suave customer whose order he was taking at that moment had his fingertip lodged just inside the gorgeous girl beside him.

Sarah averted her eyes from the barman to hide her secret shame, and was mortified to spy an elderly gentleman studying them intently. His attention was on her legs, and where Casswell's arm disappeared between their two bodies. She groaned quietly with despair.

'We're being watched,' she whispered, reddening furiously.

Casswell's expression did not falter. 'I've already told you, Sarah, you may speak only when spoken to.'

Sarah tensed as his fingers idly stroked the contours of her sex. 'But...' her voice faded as she caught his eye and quickly looked down, hoping he would take it as a gesture of apology.

Casswell checked the gentleman for himself, and then moved closer still. 'Why don't we show our friend what it is he's so desperate to see?' he whispered, and before Sarah could protest he lifted her skirt. The exposure, though lasting no more than a split second, was total, and emblazoned upon Sarah's mind; an image of her sex being displayed for the old lecher by Casswell's fingers.

The gentleman smiled and lifted his glass in silent salute. Casswell acknowledged him with a nod, and then turned his attention back to his wine and his flustered companion.

Sarah could feel the old man's eyes upon her. She could almost taste his expectation, and longed for the waiter to come and tell them their table was ready. She could hardly believe what was happening to her, and wondered again if it was all one bizarre dream.

The waiter appeared at Casswell's shoulder, giving her some relief from her spinning thoughts. 'Excuse me sir; table for two?'

Casswell nodded and took Sarah's hand.

The meal was undeniably superb, and Sarah gradually felt the tension easing. They ate in the elegant dining room at a secluded table, and Doctor Rigel Casswell was the perfect companion.

He completely enchanted her. He made her laugh, telling her stories about life in the dusty by-ways of the museums where he had worked. But despite his immense charm, Sarah found herself expecting something unexpected to occur at any moment, which added an extra frisson to the relationship.

When the waiter finally cleared the table and brought dessert, Casswell refilled their glasses and lifted his in a toast. 'To *my* Beatrice,' he said, his eyes glittering with a subtle mixture of mischief and desire. Sarah found it impossible to hold his searching look, and lowered her eyes demurely.

Casswell leant closer and lifted her dainty chin with one finger. 'Modesty becomes you, Sarah. But it is important that you understand your role at Casswell Hall completely. I expect you to be my companion and slave while you are there.'

Sarah's colour deepened as Casswell continued. 'You must understand the need for you to fulfil both roles. It is essential that you are not just attractive and compliant, but also intelligent, articulate, and well presented. I travel a great deal with my work. My colleagues and I are part of an eclectic but influential circle. Of course I will ensure you have the appropriate clothes, jewellery...' His voice faded and Sarah looked up into his eyes.

He was completely focused on her, to the exclusion of everyone else in the busy restaurant. As he lifted his glass again she realised with a start that Casswell was assuming she would stay with him until he decided otherwise. It seemed he understood only too well the potency of the spell he had woven over her.

He lightly touched his glass to hers. 'Here is to a long and *very* fruitful association,' he said.

Sarah's pulse quickened. She was only too aware that some dark part of her wanted nothing more than to remain under Casswell's debauched tutelage.

After they had eaten they drove back to Casswell Hall in companionable silence. It seemed to Sarah that they now understood each other perfectly. The daylight had already begun to fade, and in the glow of the late afternoon sun the old house showed its gothic heritage all the more clearly. Sarah shivered as the car drew up under its shadow. The desolate country building suddenly seemed a long way from the noisy bustle of the Boar's Head restaurant.

As they crossed the unkempt driveway Casswell said, 'I have invited one of my associates over for dinner tonight. I expect you to attend. Chang will help you get ready.' His tone was clipped and formal. 'You may continue with your work until then. I have matters to attend to on the estate.'

Sarah nodded and Casswell waved her inside. She hurried across the dilapidated hallway, glad to get back to the relative comfort and isolation of the study.

The transcript of Beatrice's diary lay open on the desk beside the computer where she had left it. She picked it up without thinking and began to read, feeling instinctively that the past might offer her some kind of sanctuary.

Beatrice de Fleur was still out amongst the trees by the river, taking her master to the very edges of paradise:

...My naked breasts pressed tight against the cold leather of his waistcoat, my nipples brushing against the studded metal emblems of his house.

It seems no more than an instant before we both reached that ancient ground where all reason is lost and all that remains is pure pleasure. I cried out with delight as the first waves shuddered through me; waves of fire, waves of ice – while deep inside I could feel my lord's erupting pleasure echoing my own.

And then, just as my lord pulled away, I saw someone hiding amongst the trees. It was not Orme. It was not Usher. It was another, and my heart leapt with terror as I recognised the spy...

Sarah turned the page, already drawn back into Beatrice's intricate life and fears, and keen to know more.

...It was Michael, my mistress's serving boy and the one who had been sent to bring me to my lordship. I think of him as a boy, but I suppose he is older than me, though small for his age, with a mass of white-blonde hair.

His face peering out from between the branches of the woodland was as unmoving as the trees themselves, but I could see the lust in his eyes, and those dark pupils that coolly drank in my unquestioning obedience and my master's adultery. When he knew I had seen him, his face split into a devilish grin. I could see the triumph in his expression, and knew then that I was lost, and perhaps my master along with me.

I hesitated, unsure which course to take; should I tell my lord that we were found out? Before I could speak the decision was snatched away from me. Lord Usher called to my master through the trees, and as I looked towards the sound of his voice Michael disappeared from view, and I began to doubt that I had seen the boy at all. Perhaps it was not a human form I had seen spying on us, but a wood sprite? A satyr, or perhaps worse still, a wrath conjured up by my bad conscience?

My master set off across the grass and then smiled back over his shoulder towards me. 'Go back to the castle, lady,' he said. 'I will see you later.'

Left alone amongst the whispering trees, my thoughts awash with passion and desire, I tidied my clothes and headed back towards the castle gate. The shadows were rapidly closing in, and it seemed that now they had done with me, the men had forgotten I existed. With every step back towards the castle wall I tried to convince myself that Michael had indeed been an apparition, a trick of the light.

As I reached the edge of the trees, deep in my own thoughts, Michael leapt into my path and made me jump with surprise and fear. This was no insubstantial sprite. He pressed his face close to mine, the grin still fixed steadfastly upon his face.

'So,' he teased, 'it seems to me that the master has found himself a bold new filly to beat and ride. Did he break you to harness too?' Before I could dodge him he snatched my arms.

I shook him off. 'Unhand me, you stupid boy, or the next time the master raises his whip it will be to tan your hide,' I snapped.

The boy laughed, unaffected by my words, but then I know Michael is no fool; he knows he has seen enough to ruin me and perhaps my master too. He pulled me close, sliding his hand up under my skirts.

'Perhaps it would be best not to make an enemy of me, Bee. The mistress would, I am sure, be very interested to discover what it is that detains her husband all afternoon, and keeps her children's teacher away from her duties for so long.' He grinned, his hand working between my legs to cup the damp reaches of my sex. 'And what an example that same good girl, fresh from the abbey, sets her little charges, coming to her duties all sweated up and pawing at the ground like a mare in heat. What do you think it would be worth to keep the news from her, Beatrice? A little of this perhaps?' His finger eased into me.

I stared at him, quite unable to speak, quite unable to believe he would threaten me so terribly. Until now Michael had always struck me as strange boy, ungodly and unnatural in many ways, but not cruel or wicked. He is as pretty as any girl in the castle, and it is common knowledge amongst the servants that he is unnaturally drawn to men; burly knights and their like. So I wondered what on earth he might want from me.

I found out soon enough.

Before I could reply he forced me down to my hands and knees on the muddy path and dragged up my already filthy skirts around my waist.

He was far stronger than I had ever imagined, and held me tight so I could barely breath, much less escape, however much I struggled.

Smearing the juices from my sex deep into the secret recesses of my most unholy parts, he plunged a finger deep into my backside. The sensation took my breath away whilst my body screamed out in protest. As I began to sob he stuffed a rag into my mouth and pressed deeper still. It seems, much to my surprise, that the boy Michael is not the receiver of such masculine organs as are on offer, but the giver. Pressing down onto my back he pulled his finger out and drove his shaft deep, deep inside me; into those forbidden regions reserved only for unnatural and ungodly acts. His vigour made me shriek as he pushed himself deeper still. But, even though I was sick with revulsion, I dare not fight him in case he split my pretty little backside wide open.

He snorted and bucked above me, making me beg for clemency. The serving boy's reply was no more than a devilish laugh. Perhaps I am right about him after all; perhaps he is a woodland sprite.

'Scream all you like, my dear Beatrice,' he gasped in my ear, his breath as hot as flame on my cheek. 'No one is going to hear you. No one will come to your rescue. Your precious lord and master is already safely back in his apartments with his cousin Lord Usher and that dissolute bastard priest. We are all alone, you and I…'

Hot tears coursed down my face.

In the short time between Michael's discovering me with my master, and the time I crouched before him in the mud, everything in my life had changed. I just pray that I have not lost everything in those few brief moments. Though repellent to me, I know too that I am beholden to that evil boy.

Around me in the woodland the shadows lengthened,

or perhaps it was fear alone that made the world around me seem such a dark and unforgiving place. I have no idea how I got back to my chamber, nor where Michael went after his passion was spent. But in my heart I already know I have not seen or suffered the last of Michael and his obscene desires.

Chapter Eight

When Sarah looked up, to her total surprise, the little study was in almost total darkness, the only light coming from the computer screen and the angle-poise lamp on the desk. Under Beatrice's erotic enchantment time and even the dilapidated splendour of Casswell Hall had vanished into the background, taking with it memories of the youths in the barn and the meal at the Boar's Head.

Outside, beyond the shadows of ruined terraces, the tumbles of foliage and the lake, the evening sky was cut with bands of intense scarlet and gold light; remnants of a dramatic sunset.

Sarah stretched. Closing Beatrice's diary felt a little like waking from a vivid dream, so intense, so compelling, that the images lingered in the mind even after the sleeper's eyes were open. It took Sarah several seconds to gather her bearings. When her head had cleared and she finally got to her feet, the door to the study opened, framing Casswell's servant, Chang, in the gloom.

Sarah shivered; part of her had hoped it would be Casswell who came to collect her for dinner.

The small Oriental nodded towards the computer. 'It is time to finish your work for today. Doctor Casswell is expecting you to join him for dinner this evening.' He spoke in a precise manner. 'He has asked me to help you prepare.'

'I know.' Sarah tried to smile. She already had her suspicions as to what may be expected of her at dinner, but what worried her more at that moment was what Chang might want beforehand while they were alone. She could still feel the presence of the anal dildo in her mind, if not in her body.

Chang indicated the door. 'I have already drawn a bath for you.'

Sarah nodded and headed out into the hall. As she passed him, Chang smiled. The expression was so out of character that it looked almost uncanny on his normally impassive features, and did nothing to reassure her. For an instant she thought about Beatrice and her potential betrayer, Michael.

On the desk the transcript of the diary lay beside the computer. She could still feel Beatrice's presence, her sense of violation and pain, and wondered fleetingly if Chang was cast in the same mould as the servant Michael. There was no way of telling.

For an instant Sarah wished she could step back into the past, back into a time where she was an unseen observer, and did not have to participate in the dark game that Casswell and Chang had invited her to join.

'We don't have much time,' Chang said, beckoning to her, as if sensing Sarah's hesitation. 'The doctor's guest will be arriving soon.'

Without another word Sarah turned and followed him upstairs into the shadowy reaches of the old house. It appeared that Chang had already prepared everything for her. The bedroom was warm, a fire crackling in the hearth, while through the open bathroom door she could see the steaming tub of water and a pile of thick towels on a chair beside the basin.

'Now, quickly take your clothes off,' Chang instructed. 'It doesn't do to keep the doctor waiting.'

Sarah hesitated for a moment, and then slipped her jacket off and unbuttoned her blouse, terribly aware of her exposure as she dropped them onto the floor under Chang's unblinking stare. As she slipped her skirt off she realised she still smelt faintly of the youths in the barn. Her encounter with the two young hitchhikers seemed a lifetime ago now.

As she turned to undo her suspender belt Sarah caught sight of her reflection in the full-length mirror that dominated the bedroom. The image made her freeze for a second or two, and then she turned to drink in the details of her near nakedness. The mirror's cool eye ensnared her as it had the night before. It was like looking at a highly charged erotic print that bore very little relation to the image she had of herself. At Casswell Hall Sarah was fast becoming another person.

As the magic caught hold she posed for her own pleasure, totally unconcerned and unaware of Chang's dark eyes on her. Her skin had a delicate translucent glow. Her pert breasts looked exquisite in the soft lamplight, the nipples already gathered into tight dark rosebuds. Below the swell of her breasts and ribs her body narrowed dramatically into a slim waist, and below that her rounded hips, rich plains and curves, were emphasised by the black suspender belt. Sheer black stockings and the suspenders framed her naked sex.

The picture, caught in the soft lamplight, made her heartbeat quicken; Casswell, Beatrice, and Chang had transformed her into a sensual masterpiece.

She gasped as Chang moved silently behind her and ran a fingertip over her shoulder. 'We can do much better than this,' he said hypnotically. 'Let me get you ready.'

Sarah stiffened; it was as though he'd been reading her thoughts. He held her mesmerised gaze in the mirror while he reached around her, and his small but strong hands cupped her breasts, and then moved down to her waist and hips. It was as if he was showing her nakedness off, displaying it for the mirror's anonymous stare.

'I have found, Miss Morgan, that the slave who understands their appeal fares far better in the long run,' he said, enigmatically. He pressed closer, moving his face slowly along the sweeping contours of her neck and shoulders. His lips and nose were just a fraction of an inch above her flesh, as if he was savouring her essence.

'You smell,' he suddenly said flatly, flashing an accusatory glare at her via the unrelenting mirror. 'Men... sweat... semen. What whorish things did you do this afternoon?'

Sarah shuddered and looked away, reddening furiously. Oh, what shame she felt. She wished the floor would swallow her up.

Chang laughed, the sound making her flesh creep.

'Who was it?' he persisted, idly circling one of her shamefully erect nipples with a fingertip. 'Someone staying at the hotel, perhaps? Or did Doctor Casswell pick them up on the road? He does like to test his converts' obedience at an early stage.'

Sarah swung round to face her tormentor. 'I think I'd like to have my bath now,' she said, with more defiance than she really felt.

'Well, of course,' Chang snorted with mock deference. 'Whatever my lady wants.'

With some reluctance she accepted his offered hand

and allowed him to lead her into the bathroom.

The capacious claw-foot bath was generously filled with soothingly perfumed water. It was with relief that Sarah climbed in and let the water embrace her, relishing its gentle caress on her tender skin and aching muscles.

Until the soft water enveloped her she hadn't realised just how fatigued she was. She sank down into the fragrant bubbles and closed her eyes. Her mind drifted for a few minutes, and then she was snatched back to reality as a firm hand skirted across her shoulders. She opened her eyes, and there was Chang, stripped to the waist and preparing to soap her inert body.

In spite of herself Sarah sighed with pleasure. He seemed to understand where the pain was without her saying a single word. It was utter luxury. Chang leant closer. 'I will wash your hair now, and then I am going to blindfold you.'

Sarah softly moaned her assent; so low was her resistance at that moment, she couldn't care what he did. She breathed deeply and wallowed amongst the fragrant suds, totally captivated by the soft insistent circling of his astute fingers.

Rigel Casswell filled his guest's glass and then lifted his own in welcome.

'It's good to see you again, Oliver. How was your trip?'

'Fine, not a problem,' replied Oliver Turner. 'It's good to be here, old man. How goes the translation? I'm looking forward to seeing the transcripts.' He paused and sipped his sherry, his eyes alight with curiosity. 'But to be perfectly honest, I'm rather more interested in your new houseguest at the moment. Tell me about the girl's training. How is she coming along?'

Casswell smiled at the elderly gentleman; without Turner's intervention and intuition he would never have found Sarah Morgan in the first place. Oliver Turner had been an acquaintance of Sarah's aunt, a lifelong patron of the museum, and had been the man responsible for suggesting that Sarah take the job in the office there.

'You were right about her. I should have trusted your judgement; after all, it has never failed me yet. She's a natural. Obviously unschooled as yet, but she'll be excellent by the time I am finished with her. A perfect companion for the connoisseur. I am certain you'll like what you see. Chang is preparing her now for us.'

Turner nodded. He was a large, plump man, with a ruddy complexion that reflected his taste for good living. Dressed in formal evening clothes he was an impressive sight. 'It will be an absolute pleasure to meet Miss Morgan again. And was she unbroken?'

Casswell eyed the rich amber liquid in his glass thoughtfully, and then smiled. 'Completely untouched, until she arrived here.'

Turner chuckled and selected a canapé from a plate on one of the side-tables. 'I see you speak in the past tense, my dear boy. Can I presume there is no need for me to ask about the state of affairs now? How is she coming along?'

There was a discreet knock on the door. 'Ah, that'll be Chang,' Casswell said. 'You'll be able to judge for yourself, Oliver.' He raised his voice to admit Chang and his beautiful charge.

The double doors swung open to reveal Sarah. Casswell couldn't quite suppress a smile of delight.

Sarah Morgan looked perfect. Flanked by candles in

the wall sconces, she was blindfolded, barefoot, and naked beneath a transparent high-necked black voile gown. Chang had dressed her hair into a soft bun with corkscrew tendrils that framed her delicate features, and as a final touch he had added a pair of diamond and pearl dropped earrings.

The scarlet lipstick on her generous mouth and the sheer black fabric of the gown seemed to emphasis the richness of the girl's creamy flesh. Around her neck Chang had fastened a black leather choker to which was attached a fine silver chain.

Her nipples had been rouged to emphasise their ripeness, and her denuded sex looked as moist and succulent as a peach; Sarah Morgan was indeed a mouthwatering feast.

As Chang led her into the dining room, Casswell was pleased to see her arms were secured firmly behind her back. A nice touch, and one that not only emphasised her vulnerability, but also thrust her breasts forward, showing them off to their best advantage.

Beside him, Casswell heard Oliver Turner let out a little grunt of appreciation.

'Very nice work, Casswell, very nice work indeed,' he said with gruff good humour, and waved to Chang. 'Bring her a little closer, there's a good fellow, and let me get a better look at her.'

Chang instantly obeyed.

Turner put a finger under the girl's chin and tipped it towards him, gently turning her blindfolded face this way and that. Sarah did not resist. Turner sniffed and glanced at Casswell. 'Do you mind?' he asked.

Casswell shook his head and smiled as though showing off his prize Bentley to a potential purchaser. 'Not at all,' he said amiably. 'Help yourself.'

Turner murmured his appreciation of his host's courtesy, and ran a speculative hand over the diaphanous material that strained to contain Sarah's breasts. She instinctively flinched away from his first light touch, so he pulled his fingers away and paused patiently while Chang harshly admonished her disrespectful behavior and warned her not to be so recusant again. When she had mumbled her apology, Turner cupped her breasts again and took evident pleasure in weighing them in his palms like ripe fruit.

'I prefer my fillies to be a little heavier, with a tad more meat on their bones. But I cannot deny, she is a sumptuous piece.' He pinched her painted nipples. Sarah flinched again, but bravely held her position. The scarlet nubs of sensitive flesh stiffened traitorously between his cruel fingers and thumbs.

'She responds nicely,' Turner adjudged, licking his lips and gliding a hand down over her softly rounded belly to the mound of her sex. Sarah couldn't suppress a pleasurable sigh as his fingers delicately parted the lips of her quim through the sheer gauze. Her thighs inched apart instinctively, and Turner was able to press a finger a little way inside, his single robust digit swathed in fine black gossamer.

'Good and tight,' he decided. 'And responding nicely; she already coats my finger with juices.' Sarah blushed behind the blindfold at his utterly humiliating commentary. 'It would seem you have yourself a very good deal here, my dear Rigel.'

Casswell noted the colour rising in her cheeks. He imagined the anticipation and trepidation she would have experienced when being led down through the darkened house, bound and unable to see. The moan that danced lightly from her full lips was completely instinctive; a subtle combination of fear and desire.

Turner held out his other hand to Chang, who passed him Sarah's lead. Casswell could see that the elderly gentleman was delighted with Sarah's progress so far – and guessed what was soon to follow.

Turner gently led Sarah to one of the ornate chairs that graced the dining table, and took off his dinner jacket. Settling himself comfortably he guided her, with some discreet help from Chang, over his knees.

It was a provocative pose. Sarah looked exquisite; blindfolded with her bottom raised and her lithe body still covered by the black chiffon. Casswell sensed her anxiety. She had presumably guessed what was to follow. He wondered whether she thought it was his lap she was bent over, or had she already guessed that it was his dinner guest who was about to put her through her paces.

Oliver Turner swung back his hand and brought it down sharply across Sarah's waiting backside with such vigour and enthusiasm that the sound of flesh on flesh cracked out like a pistol shot.

Although Sarah had tensed, waiting for the blow, she arched up, shrieking in surprise. As her head lifted her breasts strained forward, nipples erect and thrusting, her mouth open in a perfect oval of astonishment and pain.

Within the dark confines of the blindfold, Sarah was stunned. The sensation of the unseen hand exploding across her backside roared through her like a tidal wave. She had no idea who her tormentor was. He smelt of pipe tobacco and she guessed he was older than Casswell. But other than that he could have been anyone... except she had the weirdest sensation that she knew him.

She strained for clues, but all she could hear with any real clarity was her own heartbeat and frantic breaths. She could sense his growing excitement, and wasn't surprised when the intimidating stiffness of his cock pressed into her belly.

After a second or two she felt the muscles in his thighs tense and knew instinctively that there was another blow on its way. If anything, this one was even harder, and the cracking contact upon her defenceless flesh wiped away every thought except an awareness of the astonishing heat and pain left in its aftermath. For a few seconds fingers lingered on her throbbing flesh, and then they were gone and she knew he intended to smack her again.

The next blow was lower, stinging across the lips of her sex. She bucked and twisted to avoid the tortuous hand, but it was impossible. Somewhere in the back of her mind she could imagine the picture she must present, both to her tormentor and to Doctor Casswell.

Sarah cried out again as the next blow hit home, her mind finally releasing the puzzle of the man's identity while every nerve ending absorbed the intensity of the plethora of sensations. There was another stroke, and then another…

Just as she began to ebb and flow with the rhythm of the pain, the stranger straightened his legs and she rolled helplessly, still blindfolded and bound, to the floor. She lay for a while in silence, without being disturbed, exhausted and breathing heavily.

Eventually unseen hands pulled the leather collar and dragged her up onto her knees. Fingers once again strayed to explore the delicious curves of her breasts. Each touch, each sensation, seemed to flood her body with light, and she wondered then if all her humanity had been stripped away, leaving only the power of feeling.

Casswell smiled as Chang lifted Sarah onto her knees. With great deliberation Oliver Turner unbuttoned his immaculate trousers and guided his bony white shaft towards the girl's unsuspecting mouth.

With one hand he caught hold of her hair and pulled her between his spread thighs, and then guided her face down towards his crotch. His gnarled erection sprouted from his open trousers and brushed her lips. She tensed and instinctively pulled away.

'Come on, girl,' Turner snorted hoarsely, pulling her closer still. 'Don't be so damned coy, or I'll have to spank you a little more.'

Sarah resisted a little longer, and then, knowing it was useless, yielded and allowed him to push her head lower. As she licked experimentally at the cock that stood before her, Chang undid her arm restraints, and to the delight of both host and guest she lifted her hands, curled her fingers around the throbbing shaft, and fed it into her mouth.

As she knelt in front of Turner, her head bobbing and the wet sounds of her suckling reaching Casswell, he could just make out the moist contours of her sex between her thighs, still veiled by the sheer black gauze. Framed by the glowing orbs of her bottom it was temptation indeed. Glancing to his side he noted that Chang too was watching Sarah's submission with interest.

Casswell understood only too well that his servant's inscrutable expression hid a multitude of dark and powerful desires. Chang, he knew from experience, was more interested in the tight puckered closure between Sarah's buttocks than the gripping confines of her quim.

It was tempting to invite Change to take advantage of Sarah's humble compliance. Had they been alone he may well have engineered it, but he knew his guest would be mortally offended, horrified even, at the very notion of sharing a girl with a mere servant. And so, accomplished and perceptive host that he was, Casswell merely refilled his glass and indicated that Chang should leave them to their pleasures. It was, after all, almost time for supper to be served.

As the door closed behind the servant, Casswell placed his empty sherry glass on the occasional table beside his armchair and dropped to his knees behind Sarah.

He smiled narrowly. Above him, Oliver Turner, his ruddy face set with a look of hedonistic determination, was clearly relishing every caress from the girl's tongue and lips. His hips lifted and ground furtively as he closed his eyes and pressed down on the back of her head.

Raising the soft film of Sarah's evening dress, Casswell ran a hand over those creamy white buttocks, their pallor emphasised by the crimson marks of the spanking severely administered by Turner. Sarah trembled and twitched under his caresses, but obediently did nothing to resist. He wondered if she guessed it was him kneeling behind her, though deep down he knew she did.

She pressed back towards him, her thighs parting a little wider as he gently teased her. He smiled; the way she moved beneath his fingertips was no flirtation, but an instinctive response; a subconscious invitation to proceed.

Without further ado he accepted that invitation. He undid his fly, lifted out his aching cock, and eased it deep inside her. When fully embedded he listened to her groaning around his host's cock, and watched the expression of astonishment and ecstasy etched on the elderly gentleman's face. He held her narrow waist with one hand, guiding her slowing back and forth on his sleekly coated erection, and sought her erect clitoris with the other.

As he found the sensitive hood she shuddered. Turner snorted and Casswell pressed harder against the gently gyrating bottom of the sandwiched girl.

Sarah Morgan really was everything Casswell could ever have hoped for – and more. Her body closed tightly around him like a hungry mouth.

Hungry… and oh so desperate for satisfaction.

Chapter Nine

Under the circumstances, dinner went remarkably well. Sarah recognised Oliver Turner as soon as her blindfold was removed, but the gentleman, now his desire and curiosity were sated, was charm itself. Helping himself to another sherry, he asked after her welfare and made small talk as if he was some kind of benign godfather, rather than the man who had procured her sexual services for Rigel Casswell.

She wondered what he had seen in her; what dark ingredient in her character had given her away to him? But her sense of recognition was mingled with feelings of betrayal. Oliver Turner, if not exactly a family friend, had been a trusted acquaintance, and yet he had directed her knowingly towards this strange encounter with Rigel Casswell. It was odd; she tried to weigh up her feelings. She wasn't sure whether she felt outraged that he had decided she would be perfect for Casswell's tastes, or delighted that he had helped her find her true nature. The paradox was uncomfortable.

Casswell poured Sarah a glass of wine and invited her to join him beside the fire. As their eyes and fingertips met he smiled. It appeared that the Doctor was genuinely pleased with her performance. Sarah took a deep breath, and as she accepted the glass she murmured her thanks. Her heart was still beating out a tattoo, and between her thighs she could feel the remnants of Casswell's pleasure mingling with her own. It took her a little while to compose herself, but the two men seemed totally oblivious to any embarrassment or discomfort and began to talk as if nothing out of the ordinary had happened. She shivered as she realised that was exactly how they viewed the recent events.

The atmosphere in the dining room was remarkably convivial. As they took their places at the table, it struck Sarah that they could all quite easily be in a private club or a restaurant. The dark wood panelling, the log fire crackling in the grate, and the orange light from the flames reflecting in the chandelier above all combined to evoke an older more decadent age.

Sarah's fingers tightened around her glass and she took a long sip of her drink. She must try and remember what Casswell had told her at the hotel, when he had toasted her as his Beatrice. Her role in his life was to be both as companion and slave.

Sarah settled herself at the table next to Casswell, eyes demurely averted as Chang served their first course. Taking up his soup spoon, Oliver Turner rapidly turned his attention and the conversation to a trip he and a group of companions had recently taken to New York. He seemed completely oblivious to the fact that Sarah was naked under the sheer black gown; his thoughts had already moved on.

At last, as the wine and good food began to take effect, Sarah felt herself starting to relax. On either side of her the two men talked about the real world out beyond the magical enchantment of Casswell Hall. Sarah realised that in a matter of a few days she had almost forgotten about her life outside the walls of Casswell's fading mansion.

As Chang refilled her glass she could hear Casswell's

words from earlier in the day echoing in her head: *'It is essential that you are not just attractive and compliant, but also intelligent, articulate, and well presented. I travel a great deal with my work. My colleagues and I are part of an eclectic but influential circle. Of course I will ensure you have the appropriate clothes, jewellery...'* It seemed that tonight was part of her initiation into that charmed circle.

Sarah looked up into his eyes. To her delight he smiled at her and lifted his glass in salute, while across the table Oliver Turner began to wax lyrical about the acquisition of some important artefacts by a small gallery both men knew well. She felt the desire arcing between them; a spark of electricity, unseen by Turner. She shivered and looked way, afraid of the intensity of emotion that Rigel Casswell lit in her.

The meal itself was delightful and the two men and their friends appeared to live a fascinating life. Sarah was happy to listen to their tales of expeditions and explorations, of finds and obscure facts. Finally, after coffee and liqueurs, Casswell suggested that Turner join him for cigars and brandy in the billiard room, and as the two men got to their feet, Sarah realised she was being dismissed for the evening. The abrupt end to their soiree took her by surprised, and she wondered, given the secrecy surrounding the translation of Beatrice's dairy, whether there were things they wanted to discuss alone.

Oliver Turner bade her goodnight by kissing her on the forehead, re-enforcing the impression that he was a benign old godfather. Casswell stood over her and lifted her fingers to his lips, then nodded towards Chang, who stood at her shoulder like a bodyguard.

'Thank you,' he said, his eyes dark and unfathomable. Sarah wondered whether he was thanking her or his inscrutable housekeeper.

When Doctor Casswell had left the dining room with his guest, Chang caught hold of her arm. 'You did very well tonight,' he purred. 'He is proud of you.'

Something about the little man's tone made Sarah shiver.

He continued, 'But now they've done with you, left like a discarded toy, abandoned until they are ready to play again. I should warn you that the doctor and his friends are easily bored. But it is a shame to have to go back to your room alone. It isn't late…'

Sarah stared at him. It was the most he had said to her since she arrived at the hall. His tone was almost conciliatory. She wondered what he was suggesting and then gasped with shock as he caught hold of the chain on her collar and jerked it sharply so that their faces were no more than a fraction of an inch apart.

She could smell the sweet burr of alcohol on his breath, and looking into the dark bottomless pools of his eyes she wondered if he was jealous of her involvement with Casswell. The chain tightened a little and she realised that, once again, she was at the mercy of the little man.

'What had you in mind?' she asked, struggling to retain some semblance of composure.

Chang laughed without humour. 'I can see why the good doctor was and is attracted to you. What happened to the rule of silence, Miss Morgan? Have you learnt nothing while you've been here? I have been having supper downstairs with a close friend of mine, perhaps you would care to join us for a little after dinner drink?'

Sarah found it impossible to suppress a shudder. She

guessed he was drunk, and although the Oriental's words constituted a polite invitation, the tone did not.

'What is it you want from me, Chang?' she said, trying to sound firm, but the apprehension reflecting in her voice.

'Total obedience, and total silence unless given permission otherwise; much the same as the doctor.' He smiled, but there was no warmth in the smile. 'I have a very similar outlook to Doctor Casswell when it comes to women.' He wrapped the chain purposefully around his fist. 'Come with me, my friend is eager to meet you.'

The journey down through the old house, with Chang holding the chain tightly and tugging her along, was almost more than Sarah could bear. It felt as though she was being dragged down into the bowels of hell. The house was dark, with dim pools of lamplight punctuating the gloom. Away from the fire's warm glow it was bitterly cold and the neglect and decay more obvious. Sarah shivered, though not just from the icy chill.

Finally, at the end of a gloomy passageway, Chang opened a door and pushed Sarah into a large dingy kitchen, warmed by an old-fashioned range. A large scrubbed table dominated the centre of the room. Sitting in a Windsor chair, between the black-leaded stove and the kitchen table, was a big Nordic-looking man dressed in a grey uniform. A bottle of brandy and two glasses stood alongside a peaked cap on the table. Sarah guessed Chang's visitor must be Oliver Turner's chauffeur, and perhaps his bodyguard. Whatever, the man was a giant in comparison to the diminutive Oriental.

As Sarah was tugged into the warm room the muscular blonde lifted a brandy balloon in greeting and got to his feet. 'Good evening,' he said, extending a hand, 'you must be Miss Morgan. My name is Oscar. I have heard a great deal about you.'

Sarah swallowed hard, horribly aware of her nakedness under the sheer black gown as his powerful hand closed around her dainty one. He looked her up and down, and then moved a little closer, as if to inspect what was on offer. He stood head and shoulders above her, and although heavily muscular, he moved with an effortless grace.

'Very nice,' he said to Chang, who was busy refilling the glasses with brandy. Sarah blushed as he circled her, looking but not touching. His eyes moved down over her body meticulously, as if he was afraid he might miss some tiny vital detail. In some ways Oscar's coolly analytical appraisal of her body was far more invasive than any caress. She shivered, her discomfort intensifying as he prowled behind her. He was so close she could feel his breath on her skin.

Eventually, the inspection over, the blond pulled a cigar from an inside jacket pocket and lit it, before nodding his approval. He sat down in the chair and grinned across at Chang.

'The quality of your table scraps is really quite astonishing, my friend,' Oscar said, his English excellent but his accent heavily Germanic. He raised the cigar and drew upon it over-elaborately as if to prove his point. 'A fine Havana, a very decent brandy, and a good woman. I am extremely impressed.'

He smiled broadly, showing two rows of neat white teeth, and beckoned Sarah closer. She felt powerless to resist him, and stepped hesitantly towards the chair. Oscar reached up and ran his fingertips over her throat, and then gripping her chin very gently, he pulled her flushed face down to his. He brushed her lips with his lips, his touch so delicate that Sarah gasped with surprise.

The man's deep blue eyes twinkled with mischief. 'Not all men just take what they want, little one,' he whispered seductively, his tone lower now and more intimate. 'There are other ways that are equally as effective. Chang tells me you are being trained to serve your master, Doctor Casswell.'

His hands gently cupped her face and he kissed her again, this time his tongue insinuating itself between her lips. His touch was rekindling her desire, and she was stunned to realise she was trembling with anticipation. This was a lover's caress – a seduction – completely at odds with almost everything else she had experienced at Casswell Hall.

'Well,' Oscar asked as he pulled away and stood up, 'is it true? Are you learning to be a slave? Are you learning to be totally obedient, to submit to whatever is demanded of you?'

Sarah struggled to find her voice.

The tall blond smiled again, his expression encouraging a response. As Sarah watched he slowly unbuttoned his uniform jacket, slipped it off, and carefully hung it over the back of his chair. He then removed his white shirt, and as Sarah gazed at his impressively muscled torso she wondered into what honeyed trap she had unexpectedly strayed.

Her eyes were drawn magnetically to his slab-like pectoral muscles, and she gasped at the sight of each nipple, pierced with an ornate silver ring. The very idea made her shiver.

'Well,' Oscar prompted again, stroking a stray curl from her brow, 'are you Casswell's slave girl?'

She nodded, mesmerised by his beautiful body. The quietly watching Chang was forgotten. 'Yes... I suppose I am,' she whispered, and then looked up into Oscar's eyes. To her surprise she saw not derision, but understanding, and knew then that in his way he too was a slave of his master's passion.

'I came here to work as a secretary,' she continued, 'but I know now that's not why Doctor Casswell invited me here.'

Oscar motioned her away. 'Good. Why don't you take off your dress. It would be a shame to spoil something so pretty.'

Sarah stiffened at his assumptive bearing. It seemed any respite was to be short-lived.

Oscar pulled a face. 'Come along, Sarah, I won't hurt you. I will give you only pleasure – I promise. Trust me. Here, let me show you.'

Before she could protest or prevent him he began to undress her, with Chang hovering in the shadows and clearly enjoying the role of voyeur. The chauffeur's touch was as light as a feather as he unfastened the tiny buttons at the back of the gown. She seemed to be naked in an instant; the exquisite black voile dress sliding down into a pool around her ankles. Gently, Oscar lifted her up onto the table. She was powerless to resist him; she actually craved his considerate ministrations, so alien did they now seem.

He stood between her parted legs, looking down at her. 'Trust me,' he said again, and then kissed her gently on the mouth. She shivered and closed her eyes, surrendering herself entirely to the tall chauffeur's caresses. The heat of his body moving against hers made her ache, while his tongue and lips worked down over her throat and shoulders. As she strained to accept his caresses, his knowing fingers began to stroke the naked lips of her sex.

Sarah gasped at his subtlety and his gentleness. His lips and tongue sucked and caressed each nipple in turn, her ribs, her navel, and when his tongue finally found her clitoris she cried out her pent-up joy.

Urging her pelvis up to meet Oscar's tongue, her fingers entwined in his thick blond hair, she wondered if it was possible to die from sheer pleasure. Oscar aroused her with an expertise she never dreamed anyone capable of. He took her again and again to the very brink of orgasm and then, just as she was about to tumble headfirst into oblivion, he was skilled enough to snatch her back, until she was writhing deliriously from a heady mix of frustration and ecstasy.

'Please... take me there... please...' she moaned, in her delirium unable to find the words to describe the release she craved so desperately. 'Set me free... make me come... please...!'

Sarah and Oscar were being watched. Not just by Chang, but also by Doctor Rigel Casswell and Oliver Turner, who had taken up two comfortable chairs amongst the faded splendour of Casswell's billiard room.

Strategically placed around the large old house, and undetectable to the casual observer, were a number of hidden cameras, part of a state-of-the-art security system that had been installed. Not only did the system offer an excellent way to keep a constant vigil on the hall's very unusual collection of treasures, it was also the perfect toy for the dedicated voyeur. Behind a sliding panel, one wall of the billiard room was lined with a bank of television screens.

Casswell poured his guest another drink. 'Your man was a good find,' he said conversationally.

Turner nodded. 'Indeed, my intuition has seldom let me down. I found him in a brothel in Hamburg, you know, working as doorman-cum-handyman. Gentle as a lamb, and a wonderful seducer of the reluctant, whether they be male or female. It seems it's all the same to Oscar. And the boy is always such a pleasure to watch at work, although to be frank, perhaps a little too pedestrian for my tastes these days.

'And what about your chap, Chang? He's been with you for some years now, hasn't he?'

'Indeed he has,' Casswell confirmed. 'I found him in Hong Kong when I was a delegate on a cultural conference, back in the eighties.'

Casswell directed Oliver Turner's attention back towards the viewing screen. Sarah, legs spread wide, was writhing on the table with the blond chauffeur's head buried deep between her thighs. She thrust up towards him again and again with her fingers tugging at his hair, clearly chasing the moment of release. Her breasts rose and fell majestically as she breathed deeply, her mouth open, her eyes tightly clamped as the waves of pleasure washed through her. Her growing excitement was so all engulfing that Casswell could almost feel it himself. But what had really attracted his attention was that behind the blond giant the naked Chang was moving closer.

At some unseen signal Oscar pulled away, his face glistening with the girl's copious juices. She moaned her frustration, but his skilful lips and tongue were quickly replaced by his equally skilful fingers, and she writhed and moaned anew.

As if choreographed, Oscar slipped off his trousers and climbed up onto the table beside her. She reached for him, and as she did he adeptly rolled her up and on top him.

To the watching Casswell's delight she threw back her head and shrieked with utter delight as she found the chauffeur's rigid penis. In the half-light it boasted generous dimensions, the foreskin pierced by a heavy silver ring that matched those in his nipples. Despite the ornament, Sarah did not hesitate. She gripped the column of flesh as though fearful of losing it, manoeuvred herself over his groin, and sank onto him with a long sigh of relief and joy.

Casswell smiled. Sarah's graceful body had a compelling fluidity. She was at her most compliant. Her sex was so moist that the area where their bodies coupled glistened through the gloom.

It was a real delight to see the young man's penis pumping up and down between the naked lips of her quim. And then quietly, on silent feet, Chang climbed onto the table behind the lovers and took his place between their thighs.

If she detected his presence she gave no signs, but Casswell knew exactly what the little Oriental had on his mind. Sarah Morgan was so awash with passion, so far along the route toward oblivion that Casswell doubted if she knew her own name. While Oscar tightened his grip on her, pulling her closer to him, Chang ran a speculative finger across the puckered rosebud between her pale buttocks. Sarah stiffened for an instant – but it was her body now, not her intellect or reason that was guiding her, and as the host and guest sat silently and watched, her body opened like a flower and accepted Chang's dark caress.

With relative ease the little Oriental pushed a straightened finger home, and as he did he smeared Sarah's delicate flesh with the rich fragrant juices from her coupling with Oscar.

Chang's finger aped the rhythm of the lovers, echoing Oscar's deep thrusts, and then, at the peak of the arc, he slipped his finger out and nuzzled his cock against the same tight entrance. Sarah visibly stiffened and held her breath, and then slumped onto the large chest beneath her as Chang eased into her fully with one long thrust.

As Chang's hollowed buttocks moved slowly back she arched up again, her eyes closed, and moaned her delight. Oscar's fingers slid down over her taut belly and began to caress the wet folds of her quim, as if to calm her. It was enough. Sarah began to buck and roll her head, twisting back and forth as wave after wave of orgasm washed over her like a stormy ocean. And as she surrendered to the storm clouds of oblivion, she carried first Oscar and then Chang with her into the very depths of the ocean of desire.

Casswell closed his eyes and savoured the unforgettable image of such animalistic passion. In his mind he fed from them, replenishing his dark desires. His pulse raced. On many occasions he had shared a woman with Oliver Turner, and he knew only too well how contagious the extreme sensations could be as they rolled between each of the players.

Turner grunted his own approval of the show before him. 'It would appear this time, my dear Rigel, you may well have your new Beatrice,' he said with a grim smile, his unblinking eyes never deviating from the screen.

Casswell nodded with quiet satisfaction. 'I've been thinking much the same, Oliver. All in all, she is an excellent find – and I thank you for that. Now, what say you we have that game of billiards I promised?'

Casswell refilled his own glass, as on the screen the satiated performers began to disentangle themselves. Although the doctor was loathed to admit it, to himself or anyone else, he was envious of the young chauffeur for making Sarah so tender... so eager.

As Chang finally led Sarah back to her bedroom, a vivid impression of Beatrice hurrying back through the woods to the castle filled her mind. It seemed that amongst both their duties was the role of compliant sex slave to any number of their masters' servants.

Sarah glanced at the inscrutable Oriental. Tonight her body had given him the thing he craved most of all, even though her mind had not – initially, at least – been quite so willing. As he opened the door to her room she was aware that at some level they too were kindred spirits; both served Casswell without question, and both had to share his secret passions. She wondered if there would ever be a time when he might be an ally.

As they reached the bed she searched his eyes for any sign of a bond between them, but Chang's expression was as impassive and unfeeling as ever. She shivered, and did not resist as he made her lie down and fixed the chain he led her by to its sturdy frame.

It would have been fairly simple, had she wanted, to free herself. Chang's action was really no more than a gesture, but even so, it was a potent one.

Chapter Ten

Through the long night Sarah dreamt she was Beatrice, running between the contorted trees of a dark and stormy forest. Exhilarated by the chase, her pulse beat like a drum. Close behind her, Chang was in pursuit, carrying the leather collar and lead, while behind him ran Oscar, exquisitely naked, beautiful, bounding like a stag through the dense undergrowth, his powerful cock swinging between his muscled thighs.

As she dodged left and right between low branches and fallen trunks, Sarah felt that Rigel Casswell and Oliver Turner were hidden somewhere close by, watching her every move, and ultimately it would be them rather than Chang or Oscar who would catch her...

When Sarah finally opened her eyes, daylight was streaming in through the open curtains, and to her surprise Chang was arranging a tray of tea on the bedside cabinet. It was the sound of him moving around that had woken her. She studied him through sleepy eyes. The contrast between his role as servant and the events of the night before could hardly be greater.

Sarah arched her back and stretched, aware of the chain still fastened to the bed. She smiled at her enigmatic companion. 'Good morning,' she sighed, natural good manners overcoming all other emotions.

'Good morning,' he returned flatly. 'Doctor Casswell will be going out later. He expects you to accompany him. I will run you a bath and assist you in your preparations.'

'Where are we going?' she asked. 'What time will he expect me—?'

'I have already told you,' he snapped before she could finish, 'you talk too much! Where I come from a chattering concubine would have her tongue cut out! Any loss of pleasure is more than compensated for by the delight of their unquestioning silence!'

Sarah gasped at his belligerent outburst. If he had meant to shock her he had certainly succeeded.

'The sooner you learn to speak only when spoken to the better,' he concluded cruelly. 'Now, you will bathe, and then you will breakfast. There is time for you to continue your work this morning, before the doctor leaves for his meeting. When you have washed and eaten I will help you dress.'

Sarah decided it would be wise to do as she was told without further comment. Her thoughts were firmly fixed on his unexpected outburst and his unnecessarily threatening attitude. It was hard to fathom exactly what he was truly thinking – or what he was truly capable of. All she knew with any certainty, was that it would be in her best interests to do as he told her.

It was nine-thirty when Chang led Sarah downstairs to the study. A fire roared and spat in the grate. Everything appeared to be exactly as she'd left it. She switched on the computer and settled herself comfortably at the desk. In some ways, despite the familiarity of the objects around her, it felt as if months had passed since she had last visited the beleaguered slave girl and her master.

Sarah picked up Casswell's file, and then, looking at her transcript on the screen, re-read the last few lines of the previous day's work. In an instant she was catapulted back into the events at the castle. Beatrice had been trapped in the woods by Michael, and as the darkness crept towards them, the dense trees deadened the sounds of the slave girl's fears:

…'Scream all you like, my dear Beatrice,' he gasped in my ear, his breath as hot as flame on my cheek. 'No one is going to hear you. No one will come to your rescue. Your precious lord and master is already safely back in his apartments with his cousin Lord Usher and that dissolute bastard priest. We are all alone, you and I…'

Hot tears coursed down my face.

In the short time between Michael's discovering me with my master, and the time I crouched before him in the mud, everything in my life had changed. I just pray that I have not lost everything in those few brief moments. Though repellent to me, I know too that I am beholden to that evil boy.

Around me in the woodland the shadows lengthened, or perhaps it was fear alone that made the world around me seem such a dark and unforgiving place. I have no idea how I got back to my chamber, nor where Michael went after his passion was spent. But in my heart I already know I have not seen or suffered the last of Michael and his obscene desires…

Sarah hastily turned the page, wondering if now that Michael's lust was satisfied he would leave Beatrice alone, although she knew in her heart that was unlikely. With her fingers poised above the keyboard, she read on:

...Today began as bright as any this season. My master and his cousin, the Lord Usher, announced – even before we had time to break our fast – that they intended to take my lord's sons out to join them in the hunt. But even as my master stepped down into the chamber my heart fluttered with desire, and I looked away for fear of blushing and betraying all I that feel for him.

As he and the rest of his entourage turned to leave, he beckoned me closer and caught hold of my arm, tipping my face up towards his, recklessly, as if he didn't care who might see us together.

My cheeks flamed wine-red.

'I want you to come to my chamber as soon as we return,' he said. 'I would have you read a little to amuse me, Beatrice.'

With all my heart I heard the need and the desire in every last word, and feared that others might hear it too.

I nodded and curtseyed deep. 'As you please, sire.'

He smiled, and I saw the passion in his dark eyes. God preserve me from such thoughts, such hunger as coursed through my veins at that moment.

The little boys' noisy and excited departure left me with the family's two daughters, Alice and May, who were well pleased to be rid off their boisterous brothers, with all their noisy and mischievous rough and tumble.

I thought to suggest that the girls and I spend the remains of the morning at our embroideries. when I saw to my horror that Michael had been watching me from the shadows of a slightly ajar door. He beckoned me closer.

'What do you want, master Michael?' I asked, in as civil a tongue as I could manage.

The boy leered at me. 'Not I, pretty Beatrice. Oh no,

113

not I. It appears that your fame is spreading. The mistress wants to see you in her apartments as soon as you have settled the girls with their nursemaid.'

I stared at him. In some ways my mistress has always seemed a distant figure in the life of the castle, more removed, more remote, more formal than his lordship. She spends much of her time following a pilgrim's path. Since I arrived, thrice now she has been on long pilgrimages to the great shrines.

So, it did not bode well that she summoned me to her chambers. The children's nurse, Aggie, has many times told me that my ladyship was a woman who should never have married. If it weren't for her father's insistence she would most likely have taken the cloth and spent her days in the cloister behind a convent wall.

She is a dour woman, despite a strong-boned beauty, and in middle age her ladyship's face has settled into hard lines and her blue-grey eyes are as cold like flint. In the dark of the night I have often wondered about the couplings between my lord and lady. Was there ever any passion mixed with their sense of duty that fuelled their desire? I cannot imagine my master ploughing that particular furrow with any sense of relish.

But enough; my thoughts are wandering. Michael was still there in the chamber watching me, his eyes fixed on me like a hound on a hare.

'It doesn't pay to keep her waiting,' he goaded with a sneer. 'I'll tell you that for nothing.'

Once I was certain that the girls were safely closeted with their nurse I set off through the narrow passageways of the castle towards my lady's apartment in the east tower. Michael led the way, as if there was some possibility that I did not know where I was going, though with each step my heart grew heavier and heavier as I considered what might lie in store for me. What spiteful tales had the upstart servant told?

As we reached the great oak door that divides my lady's chambers from the rest of the castle, I was horrified to find that Arturo, my master's man-at-arms, was awaiting our arrival on the landing.

'Well, well… what is it we have here?' he said with a sly grin as he took my arm in a painful grip and led me into the anteroom. 'A whore? A pretty little painted trollop who repays a noble kindness with adulterous seduction? Have you any idea what the punishment is for adultery, oh corrupter of the sacred marriage bed?'

I could scarcely believe what I was hearing, and felt my pulse quicken with fury. Rounding on the vile brute, I snapped, 'If there is a corrupter here it is not I, Arturo, as you well know. You and that bastard priest—'

Arturo laughed heartily in my face, his evil eyes fixed upon me. 'Oh, how very little you know of the realities of life, my dear little slut. The truth would be of little importance to an angry mob. The heathen peasants would only be interested in how things appear. How they would crave to get their hands on that pretty little body of yours.' His eyes crawled up and down my transfixed body, and he licked his thin lips with a serpent's tongue. 'Mmm, I will take the greatest of pleasure in seeing the arrogance beaten out of you, Beatrice. And when you are broken – truly broken – I have been assured you will be mine to do with as I please…' he sniggered as his eyes fixed themselves on my heaving breasts, 'and you would not like that.'

I stepped back in terror. 'W-what do you mean?' I whispered.

'Enough of this!' snarled a female voice from close by. I span on my heel and saw, to my horror, that my lady was watching our exchange. And to my astonishment her eyes, usually so cold and unfeeling, were aglow with an inner fire that quite unnerved me.

'Strip her and let us proceed immediately with the punishment,' she snapped, waving to Arturo. 'There is much to do.'

Before I could protest or defend myself Michael and Arturo had grabbed my arms and ripped away the bodice of my gown. I screamed out in indignation and humiliation, fighting to cover my nakedness, but no amount of pleading or begging would stop them. Their bloodlust was truly up, and I was their prey!

Arturo snapped a set of manacles around my wrists and secured me like a bitch to a chain that hung from the ceiling. He pulled down with all his might, and my arms were hauled upwards until I my toes barely touched the cold floor, completely helpless to their evil approaches. Crouching at my feet, with a triumphant glint in his eye, Michael bound my ankles together.

Exposed and totally at their mercy I begged them to stop, calling on all the saints for assistance in my time of need – but perhaps my sins were too great for divine intervention.

'For God's sake silence her whining,' hissed her ladyship. 'Make haste with a gag, before the tart attracts any unwanted attention!'

She approached me then, her fine clothes presenting a stunning contrast to my raw nakedness. I hung from the rafters like a side of mutton, swinging this way and that, my arms screaming their protestations as the two men finally stripped away the last remnants of my clothes.

She grasped my hair viciously and pulled me towards her. 'I want you to understand that this is just the beginning, Beatrice. Your vile betrayal of my Christian charity cuts like a knife. If it were not for Arturo – who seems to think you will make an interesting bed companion – I would have your worthless carcass thrown to the rabble with nothing more than the clothes you stood in.'

She smiled thinly, but there was no amusement there.

'You little whore,' she hissed, quietly. 'Let you ply your chosen trade amongst the farmers and the tradesman, the sailors and the scum down at the docks… slut!'

She drew back her hand and slapped me hard across the cheek. Her face flushed with a disturbing mixture of anger and excitement.

'For some reason Arturo seems to think you have some worth. So whatever follows is thanks to him; a punishment for your adultery rather than expulsion from the castle.'

She fell silent for a few moments – deep in thought as she studied my face in a disturbing manner that made me shudder. Her eyes became misty.

'And when he is done with beating you,' she eventually continued, 'you will give me what I long for… what I deny myself…' Her mood swung again and she spat, 'You little Jezebel! You unnatural harlot!'

I stared at her ladyship in disbelief of what I was witnessing, and then shivered with utter horror and revulsion as she wrapped a wiry arm around my waist, pulled me close, and kissed me hard, her tongue driving furiously between my lips. She cupped my breasts, her long fingernails outlining the taut peaks of my nipples.

As she pulled away, the both of us breathing heavily – me from shock and disgust and she from, I know not what – the look in her eyes was as sinister and intense as the wildest darkest storm in the forest.

I had barely time to consider the implications of these most unnerving of caresses before Arturo snatched a horsewhip from his belt and swept it down like a streak of white-fire across my back.

I howled as the unjust agony bit into by flesh. My body twisted like a bizarre puppet dancing to the tune of its sadistic puppeteer. My lady had said that Arturo meant to break me, and I knew now that she truly meant it. It seemed no quarter was to be given. As I spun around and writhed in vain attempts to avoid his spite, he hit me again. This time the crop caught me full across the breasts, lifting a broad welt on my sensitive bubbies and making me wail like those who had lost their minds and were condemned to spend their days rotting in the madhouse.

As I recovered a degree and tried to twist away from the next excruciating cut my lady's eyes narrowed and darkened, and I saw there, in their depths, the evil pleasure simmering in her very soul. So this was the secret passion that drove her.

I do not know for how long Arturo beat me, nor how many strokes exploded across my hapless flesh. It seemed to continue for an eternity, my mind ablaze with pain and fear until finally my body surrendered and my senses were too overwhelmed to feel anything more. My conscious mind retreated into a dark corner where the sound of the whip and the crack of leather on flesh became abstract – almost unrelated to me.

When Michael and Arturo finally cut me down I fell

forward onto my hands and knees, exhausted, all passion, all humanity thrashed from me. I wanted nothing more than to curl into a ball and let the tender sanctity of sleep claim me. One of them tugged my head up by my hair and pulled the gag from between my limp and dry lips, while the other cut through the ties that bound my ankles.

Across the room her ladyship was arranged on a day-bed. Her bodice was undone to the waist, and her skirts lifted to reveal the dark triangle of her sex.

She beckoned me closer with a thin finger.

'First,' she purred, in a voice that came straight from all the demons of hell, 'you will suckle me. You will lick and draw at my pretty little dugs, take them deep into your mouth, and use your whorish tongue to excite them. And then you will kiss me here...' the same thin finger traced the fissure where the lips of her sex met. 'I want you to show me what pleasure, what joy, is it that has drawn my husband and Arturo under your sluttish spell.'

She paused, clearly seeing my fear and revulsion. Her expression was grim. 'You will do as I command, girl, and you will do it now, or I will have Arturo drag you down to the market like the bitch on heat that you are and sell your worthless carcass to the highest bidder!' Her voice crescendoed as the threat reached its end, and I silently wondered for her sanity. 'Do I make myself perfectly clear?!' she screamed, like one possessed.

Before I could reply she snatched my arm with a strike as quick as any snake, and pulled my face towards her breasts. They were heavy pendulous sacks, etched with faint blue veins like the roots of a tree, and tipped by crinkled dark brown nipples. I tried to resist her strength, but the beating had weakened my resolve, and I knew I had little choice but to give her all she demanded.

She cupped and lifted a breast to my lips. I ran my tongue around the dry teat, before anticipating her need and reluctantly drawing it deep into my mouth. As I struggled with my abhorrence her ladyship caught tight hold of my wrist and guided my hand to the forbidden place between her thighs. I stiffened as my fingertips brushed her clammy flesh. It was so strange to touch another woman's quim, and what disturbs me most was that mixed with my disgust and fear, was a strange and unexpected curiosity.

Her quim seemed to be alive, a sleek furred creature, and as I stroked down over its corona of curls – my caresses guided by her ever tightening grip – she opened for me, giving me greater access, pulling me into her. Her vagina, so familiar and yet so alien, was silky smooth; a glistening, moist trap. And almost without thinking I gently guided a finger into the sucking recesses. My reward was a long and throaty sigh of pure pleasure from my lady.

I am both ashamed and excited by the events that followed in my lady's chamber. For some reason her delight in my caresses, the way her body writhed against mine, made me tremble with intense and unexpected excitement.

I did not resist her guiding me; in fact, quite the opposite. As she drifted a hand across my belly, my rogue carcass lifted up to give her the access she sought; the little cherry stone that nestles between the lips of my sex.

With her example to guide me, my fingers hurried on to circle the twin of that swollen little bead between her heavy thighs, while all the time my mouth was fixed tight on her leathery nipple. She began to moan then, and thrust her hips up to my fingertips and, as she did, the scent of her passion flooded my senses, and the spark she had kindled in my belly suddenly bursting into flame.

I blush even now for thinking about what went on. My ladyship dragged my limp form up onto the day-bed alongside her and began to kiss me hungrily, one hand caressing my breasts, teasing at their swollen peaks, while her other continued to stroke and cajole the very seat of my pleasure.

I was lost.

Such sensations were a stunning contrast to the bite of Arturo's whip. My ladyship's womanly body, the way it moved and felt, was a revelation too. If I closed my eyes it almost felt as though I was making sweet love to myself.

The gentleness of her touch, and the sensation of her breath against my trembling skin, were so astonishing. No wonder such unnatural couplings are forbidden by holy writ. Black alchemy bound us. In my lady's arms I understood only too well how each of my caresses would feel for her, and within seconds of my surrender, the seduction became an intense, all-engulfing game of follow the leader. One touched, one copied. One led, one followed. The roles changed again and again as our mutual rapture mounted.

And it was undiluted rapture; this frenzied fall from grace.

When she gently pressed my head down towards her lap I offered no more than a token resistance. My mouth opened to enfold her, to drink her in. She whispered encouragement and lifted her hips. My tongue dipped again and again into the ocean of her passion – our pleasures overseen by the forgotten Arturo and Michael.

My ladyship whimpered with joy and began to move in earnest as my tongue breached her. Her back arched, her hips thrust up to meet me, and her groin buffeted my perspiring face.

I slithered to the floor between her legs to service her all the better. My lips, tongue and fingers took her to the very edge of the abyss, and as she edged closer and closer to that moment, I slid my hand down between my thighs, between my own sopping folds, and drew myself inexorably along the same wondrous path.

I felt her sex tighten around my fingers, like an avaricious mouth drawing them in. The tightening was as intense and shocking as anything I have ever felt, and as her body cocooned me my own ecstasy engulfed reason.

Above me, her ladyship thrust forward again and again and urged me on and on to greater efforts. I was exhausted, but she was insatiable.

At last there was a long, sobbing howl of release, but from whence it came is still a mystery; her soul, or mine. Such was my delirium that even to this day I know not which of us spent so passionately.

Finally there was stillness, and with it a growing sense of self-knowledge, as if I had woken from a deep and fever-soaked sleep. With the taste of her body still on my tongue and lips, shame rose and flooded my belly like the in-rushing tide. While my lady tidied herself Arturo grabbed me by the arm and pulled me roughly to my feet.

'We've not quite done with you yet,' he said softly, jerking me close to him. I could smell his excitement like sweat; watching me with her ladyship, had I sensed, been almost more than he could bear.

'Bring that iron over here,' he said to Michael, who watched our exchange over his shoulder. 'Let us ensure that Beatrice never forgets again where her loyalties lie.' I glanced over at the servant boy, and to my horror I saw he had a branding iron wedged in the grate, its end already glowing red-hot.

The young bully stooped and wrapped a cloth around the handle. As he pulled it from the white coals I realised the iron bore the lady's family crest.

There was a brief moment when I naïvely wondered as to their intentions, and as my mind formed the question, a solution struck me that seemed so preposterous I couldn't bring myself to let the notion grow. It was then I saw the look in Arturo's eyes, and knew exactly what they intended.

I tried to escape then, jerking away from Arturo's grasp, screaming, fighting him, begging, sobbing, pleading... but all to no avail. As Michael closed on me Arturo held me tight against him and her ladyship. He snatched my chin in a cruelly tight grip, tipped my head back, and from a tiny glass vial she poured something thick, red, and bitter into my vulnerable mouth and down my throat.

'Do not resist me,' my lady whispered thickly close by my ear. 'I can show you the true nature of passion. Please, dear Beatrice, do not fight what is already ordained... Drink...'

I know now that the potion was her way of easing the pain of what was to follow, but at that fearful moment the taste was so cloying and spicy, that I feared, as the liquid oozed down to my stomach, that they intended to do away with me. Their evil brand would identity my corpse.

I knew Arturo was enjoying my plight, for as I struggled against his restrictive hold I could feel his vile manhood standing proud within his breeches, and prodding insistently against my gyrating hip. As I strained against his superior strength, my lady clamped my nose and mouth tightly shut until I had finally swallowed the herbal down. When she eventually took her hands away I searched desperately for air to fill my lungs. Arturo's greedy hands taking advantage of my plight by cupping by swelling breasts as I gasped deeply did not concern me, such was my need. And then I let out a choking scream of indignation, and at that very instant Michael gleefully pressed the hot iron to one poor cheek of my bottom.

It is quite beyond my powers to describe how it felt. But even as my mind crumbled under the smell of smouldering flesh and the sensation of the heat, the dark all-engulfing trail of my ladyship's drugged potion followed close behind the ribbon of pain. The potion cut a course through my mind that was as soft as mist, and I could feel it robbing me of my senses, pulling me on towards the darkness of the abyss, until finally it closed out all thoughts...

Sarah Morgan pushed herself away from the desk. She had been holding her breath for almost all of the last two paragraphs, and she let out a strangled gasp as she reached the end of the page.

Her mind was awash with Beatrice's pain and the sense of impending unconsciousness. She shook her head to clear it and glanced up at the words her fingers had, almost unconsciously, transferred to the computer screen.

124

She wondered who else would read this account? Who else would find themselves stirred and drawn in by Beatrice's intense emotions.

Sarah sighed; it would be a terrible tragedy if the girl's story was consigned to the dry, unimpassioned halls of academe, a museum vault, or perhaps the safe of some elderly connoisseur. It seemed a tragic fate for a story so full of life and vitality.

Beatrice deserved better than that.

From out in the corridor she heard the sound of someone approaching, and guessed it would be Chang coming to get her ready for her visit with Doctor Casswell.

Chapter Eleven

Upstairs in his private apartments, Rigel Casswell, glistening with sweat, stripped off his T-shirt and jogging pants and stepped into the shower. The icy torrent of water took his breath away. Slowly, he turned up the heat and leant forward, resting his forehead and palms flat against the cool tiles, letting the water course down over his torso. The sparkling rivulets emphasised the sculptured plains of his carefully maintained body.

Naked, his frame belied his profession. No one would guess he was an academic working in a museum. His stomach was as flat as a board, and as he flexed against the tiles it revealed impressive corrugated bands of muscle. He had the body of an athlete.

Casswell stretched again, letting the water find and play over his shoulders and back. Normally after working out in the gym Chang would give him a full massage, but today there wouldn't be time. Instead, he and Sarah Morgan would be driving over to enjoy an uninterrupted view of Oliver Turner's private family museum.

Closing his eyes, he soaped familiar dips and hollows, his fingers easing across into the sore spots.

It was very tempting to imagine Sarah Morgan awaiting his command, her mind full of the passions from Beatrice de Fleur's astonishing diary. He felt a familiar stirring in his groin, and allowed himself a narrow smile. His hand, slick with soap, worked up and down the impressive arc of his cock, easing the foreskin slowly back and forth. Sarah had performed quite magnificently in the kitchen with Chang and Oliver's impressive chauffeur. He teased himself, overlaying images of Sarah's passion and pain with those of Beatrice's conversion from his own translation.

Beatrice's diary truly was an erotic masterwork; a quite astonishing find. Oliver Turner had bought it on a trip from an impoverished mid-European museum, where it had reputedly been discovered amongst the dull secular records of a religious order.

While the fabric of the diary was being subjected to scientific tests, Oliver was attempting to track the provenance of the rest of the papers. Although that in itself would prove very little; a forgery could easily be slipped amongst a bundle of authentic documents to add veracity to its origin. Sadly, it was an old trick, but even so it would help Oliver chase down the history of the rest of the documents. Casswell's job, besides making an accurate and complete translation, would be to check the family and historical references in the body of the text. It was the kind of game of detection he adored. He had always enjoyed the combination of logical deduction and intuitive leaps of faith, and was looking forward to hearing full details of Oliver's own investigations from the panel of hired experts like himself, whom Oliver had employed to work on different aspects of the diary's history.

But, despite his attempt to fill his mind with logical and historical images, Sarah and Beatrice refused to be ignored. In his imagination the two women were like celestial twins – their awakening and their stories divided only by a trick of the light.

He leant hard against the tiles and let the cascading

water play over him, adding a strange piquant beauty to his mounting desire. Sarah Morgan was like a beacon, a shining path that led him directly back to Beatrice de Fleur.

Beneath his fingertips his cock throbbed. In his increasingly excited mind both woman were gradually becoming one and the same. An erotic amalgam, so that in his imagination the woman who now awaited him was both Sarah and Beatrice. His cock ached to feel her lips around it. He ached to see her kneeling before him, a newly broken slave. Still uncertain, still a little unsure, but his nevertheless... He shivered.

Below him, in the study, Sarah would be naked beneath her smart business suit. Her denuded sex would be wet with excitement from the morning's work. And if by some chance she had decided to defy him and was wearing panties, he would punish her for such blatant disobedience, and he knew she would enjoy that too.

He would make her bend over the desk, dragging her underwear down around her knees so that she presented that plump ripe backside to him like a gift.

She would stifle a sob and beg a little as he ran a hand over her trembling flesh. His fingers would explore the wetness of her throbbing quim, and then he would turn away and prepare to mete out her punishment. The kiss of the horsewhip would help to ensure that she didn't dare disobey him again.

Casswell closed his eyes, his fingers moving rhythmically up and down the pulsating shaft of his cock. He hadn't meant to take his pleasure this far, but he had never imagined he would find a companion so much like the sensual creature of his fantasies. Of course, there had been other women before Sarah in his life – many others, in fact – but none quite like her.

As soon as Casswell had reached the age of consent Oliver Turner had taken it upon himself to direct the boy's sexual education. As his godfather, Turner had accepted it as something of a personal crusade. Under his encouraging tutelage and watchful eye, the young Casswell had sampled a rich palette of perversions and delights. Exquisite whores in Hamburg, pretty painted boys in the Far East, twin sisters in Marrakech, transsexuals in South Africa, bondage, buggery, bisexuality and every shade and shape in between. If it was there to be had, Oliver Turner had known where to find it, and as a result the boy sampled first hand innumerable delights of the flesh.

Later, when Casswell was at Cambridge, it became obvious that they both shared a certain passion for pain, and it had been then that Turner took it upon himself to introduce his protégé to whores and other men's mistresses and body slaves; women and men, willing to act out the young man's inner most fantasies. What a journey of discovery that had been. It had been a baptism of fire. Casswell closed his eyes, allowing a frenetic collage of faces, bodies and sensations to wash over him, as beneath his finger he sensed the storm was about to break.

It had been the acute understanding of his own desires that had helped him know. From the second he set eyes on Sarah at the museum, he knew she would be special. Here was a girl whom he sensed he could train to be his companion. An uncorrupted creature; a virgin, so very different from the painted whores of Amsterdam or the exquisite street girls in Bangkok. She was a paradox. Though beautiful, she was someone whose very ordinariness made her utterly extraordinary.

At her interview – arranged by Oliver Turner – Sarah had appeared so demure, so unsure of herself. And yet all the time the committee members had been talking to her, Casswell had sensed there was something more; something sensual and dark, shimmering just below the surface. It intrigued him.

Even the way she moved – a heady combination of innocence and repressed sexual energy – had made him sit up and take notice. He could see her still; ripe pert breasts pressing against the thin cotton voile of her blouse, long legs modestly crossed at the ankle and tucked under her chair, and hands folded neatly in her lap.

In his imagination she looked up at him now, her eyes alight with desire, her mouth open a little to reveal a pink tongue between full moist lips…

There was no going back now. Casswell gasped as the rip tide of pleasure roared through him, engulfing him in its current, driving away every thought but release.

His seed ricocheted across the tiles in the shower while he rode his passion out to oblivion, hanging on to his throbbing cock, milking every last sensation with his fist. Finally it was done. All passion spent, he slumped forward and dragged a molten breath into his lungs. After a moment or two he stood on slightly shaky legs and rinsed away the evidence of his secret pleasure, then shut off the water and wrapped himself in a towel.

As he strode from the dressing room into his bedroom he glanced at the clock on the mantelpiece. Somewhere close by Chang would be busy preparing Sarah for their visit to Oliver Turner's.

In the bathroom that adjoined Sarah's bedroom, Chang gently ran his hand over the mound of her sex. She was standing beside the bath, he was kneeling on the tiled floor beside her. He had spread a hair removing cream over the few days' growth that covered her quim. On his instructions she had stood very still while he applied it and remained, unmoving, waiting for it to work.

She felt self-conscious as he studied her nakedness with a casual but informed eye, as if considering bloodstock. Finally Chang looked up, and nodded.

'It is done now. Step into the shower and I will rinse you.' He offered her his hand. Sarah looked into his emotionless eyes. When, a little earlier, he had come to collect her from the study, she had offered no resistance and had followed him through the ramshackle house to her room. It occurred to her now that she had gone without question, and that she was rapidly becoming used to this new way of life, and Chang's role in it; a peculiar combination of nursemaid, servant and gaoler.

Taking the shower head down from the wall the Oriental quickly sluiced away the last remaining wisps of hair. Patting her dry he finished the job by massaging a little of fragrant oil into the rise of her quim, which made her skin feel as soft as silk. She glanced into the mist-ringed mirror on the opposite wall.

Naked, her hair was caught into a loose topknot, and dark tendrils curled by heat and steam framed her face. Her breasts where splashed with crystalline droplets of water, but it was not this that drew her attention. Chang's glistening oil drew the eyes downward to her softly rounded belly and the delicate contours of her sex below. The absence of pubic hair added a vulnerability that was quite shocking, and in an odd way made her feel and look doubly naked.

Behind her, Chang picked up a basque from the chiffonier, and while she watched in the mirror he threaded it around under her arms and settled it over her narrow waist and hips. It was odd to watch herself being dressed, and to feel it at the same time.

Made from softest black leather the basque emphasised the pallor of her skin and, as Chang tugged it tight, the beautiful hourglass contours of her body. She stared at her own reflection, transfixed by the image in the clouded glass.

The leather made the most of every curve and plain. Strapped into it, she had been transformed into a stunning sexual icon. The cups of the basque were heavily boned so that her breasts were pushed up and forward, but not covered. They presented the ripe orbs like an erotic banquet, laid out for unknown revellers to gorge themselves upon.

Gently, Chang lifted first one breast and then the other, delicately outlining the contours of each nipple with a scarlet lipstick. Sarah blushed furiously as they hardened under his touch.

The rest of her outfit consisted of sheer black stockings, high patent heels and a tailored pillar-box red coat-dress, with slightly padded shoulders and a cinched waist.

As a final touch Chang added pearl studded earrings, a little eye make-up, and a knee-weakening oval of scarlet lipstick which gave her an innocent pout which was just made to be stretched around a pistoning cock.

Sarah studied her reflection and felt her nipples stiffen. On one level she looked every inch the efficient executive's secretary, but beneath the cool exterior lurked something very different.

Chang stopped to admire his creation, and then slipped a hand up under her dress to stroke the naked lips of her quim. Instinctively, without a second thought, Sarah opened her legs for him.

Chang grinned and eased a finger into the tight moist confines of her body.

'You learn fast,' was all he said.

It was later that afternoon that Oliver Turner took Sarah by the arm and guided her along a broad corridor towards a set of impressive double doors that marked the entrance to his family's museum. Inside, the air was still and heavy, with the musty smell of old manuscripts and sun-dried dust. Glass display cabinets lined the long walls, while others were arranged in islands on either side of the central walkway.

'My great grandfather began the Turner family museum,' he said, proudly indicating a dark oil painting above them. 'He, like so many of the gentlemen of his generation, travelled widely before finally settling down. And then of course, once he began the undertaking, it set a precedent and other members of the family felt they ought to contribute items too.'

Sarah glanced back over her shoulder. Doctor Casswell was walking a pace or two behind them, looking left and right, though she suspected he wasn't actually seeing any of the bizarre collection of faded trophies and battered souvenirs. No doubt he had heard Oliver Turner's speech of introduction many times before.

She struggled to keep her attention fixed on their host's words. It seemed an extremely long way to come to explore the Turner family's moth-eaten collection of stuffed animal heads, old books, and native spears and shields.

All in all, their arrival at Oliver Turner's country estate had proved something of an anticlimax. In the car on the way she had been imagining what might happen when they finally arrived. Casswell had seemed pre-occupied, Chang drove, and so she had little left to do but daydream about what might lay in store for her. Every time she moved the black leather basque reminded her that she was near-naked beneath the elegant coat-dress. Images of her oiled sex and her rouged nipples filled her mind. It seemed as though everything had conspired to excite her.

And for what?

Beside her, Oliver Turner was still talking, '...adding his own collection of artefacts from his extensive travels in Africa almost a hundred years later...'

They had reached a set of ornate double doors, and Turner bent forward to unlock them.

'And so now to my favourite part of the collection. I have added several pieces.' He opened the doors with a flourish, and Sarah, whose attention had been wandering, gasped with a mixture of shock and complete amazement. Her first impressions of the interior and the contents of the huge room were quite overwhelming.

Inside, carefully lit and arranged around a vast circular chamber, was the most amazing collection of sexual paraphernalia she had ever seen in her life. There were masks, gags, body harnesses and suits, stocks, leg-irons, whips, great double-ended dildos, an enormous carved wooden phallus, and so much more that Sarah couldn't take it all in.

She felt her pulse quicken. The room was lined with display cabinets that no doubt held even more erotic memorabilia, but what dominated her senses was a central dais upon which stood a stunning life-sized waxwork tableau depicting an impassioned encounter between a master and his slave girl.

Under soft lighting a lithe young woman was suspended from the ceiling. Hooded, and completely anonymous, her hands were tied above her head, while her chin rested on her chest. Her skin was the colour of double cream, and her breasts, two thrusting orbs topped with large nipples, were pierced with ornate silver rings. A fine silver chain connected the two rings and glittered in the subdued lighting. It was the most exquisite and astonishing thing that Sarah had ever seen. Subconsciously she moved closer to take a look at the models, without even considering the implications of her curiosity.

The slave girl's sex was bare, and a narrow black leather thong that circled up between her buttocks and joined a studded belt divided the outer lips. To complete what was a breathtaking outfit, the model wore high black patent spiked thigh boots.

Sarah shivered, caught up in the stunning image. Was this what she looked like when bound and waiting for Doctor Casswell to lay on with the riding crop? She could feel a peculiar erotic charge surge through her veins.

'So, what do you think?' whispered Casswell, in an undertone. The sound of his voice made Sarah jump. For a moment or two she had been totally oblivious to either the doctor or Oliver Turner.

'Amazing,' she murmured thickly, and honestly. 'Absolutely amazing.'

The waxwork was at once both astonishing and deeply disturbing. Behind the slave girl crouched a small muscular man, masked too, dressed in cream jodhpurs and a dark leather jerkin. His torso was oiled, almost as if he had already worked up a lather of sweat. He cradled a horsewhip in one thick paw, and looked for all the world as if he was about to spring forward and lay on the next cruel, breath-stopping blow.

The girl was wonderfully modelled, caught in the very instant before the whip exploded across her back. Sarah could almost hear her moans of pain and pleasure, her body taut, waiting... and then she noticed something that made her suppress a gasp of horror behind her hands and step back.

The fine chain between the girl's nipples began to tremble, and then very slowly rise and fall. Sarah squeezed her hands over her mouth as comprehension dawned and nausea threatened... these weren't waxworks at all!

'M-my God!' she blurted. 'She's – she's alive, isn't she?!'

Oliver Turner laughed, and catching hold of Sarah's arm, pulled her up onto the dais.

'The game's up, my dear,' he said to the slave girl, who slipped from the restraints, pulled off the hood, and shook out a tumble of lustrous blonde curls. She moved with the easy fluid grace of a dancer, and looked almost feline.

'Bravo, my sweet,' Turner continued, pulling the girl close and brushing her cheek with his lips. He stroked one of the rings that pierced her nipples. The bud hardened instantly under his caress. 'I think we had Miss Morgan well and truly fooled for a little while.' He turned to Sarah. 'I would like you to meet my companion, Amelia. Amelia Cartwright, this is Miss Sarah Morgan.'

Sarah nodded dumbly. Unable to find her voice, she extended a trembling hand.

Amelia accepted and pulled it to her scarlet painted lips. Sarah shivered as the stunning blonde turned her hand over and ran her tongue seductively across the open palm in an all too obvious display of her inclinations toward Sarah.

'Welcome to Oliver's little museum,' she purred seductively. Her dark brown eyes were outlined with kohl, re-enforcing the impression that she was some strange exotic cat. She smiled at Sarah's obvious discomfort, and drew one of her fingers into her warm mouth. Sarah shivered.

'Oh, come on, relax,' Amelia whispered in a low, husky voice. 'Wouldn't you like to come play a little while?'

Although she was aware of Doctor Casswell and Oliver Turner standing just behind her, and beyond them the door that would lead her back into the main house, Sarah was rooted to the spot.

The blonde seducer's talons dropped, clearly not even contemplating a rebuttal, to the buttons of Sarah's dress. 'Why don't you let me see what Chang has found for you, my little darling? I'm sure it'll be something rather nice.'

One button popped free... two... three... Sarah felt her colour rising along with her temperature. The growing tension in the pit of her stomach, though not totally unpleasant, made her tremble with a heady concoction of embarrassment, uncertainty, and longing.

Amelia pouted theatrically. 'There, there. It's all right, my little one, relax and let yourself go. This game is supposed to be fun, or hasn't dear Rigel told you that yet?' She grimaced, feigning disapproval, and then glared at Casswell.

Oliver Turner sighed. 'Be careful, Amelia my dear, or I will have to take the horsewhip to you after all.'

Undeterred, Amelia chuckled sexily, and snatching the whip from the waxwork figure of the slave master, ran her hand suggestively down its black leather shaft.

'Oh, my pleasure entirely, Oliver,' she purred with a confident grin, sliding the whip between her thighs.

Oliver Turner laughed dryly. 'You are a little vixen, and no mistake,' he said.

Amelia dropped to her hands and knees, and nuzzled at the elderly gentleman's crotch while still working the crop between her thighs.

Sarah gasped at the shameless display.

Turner shook his head, and then ruffled the blonde's hair as he would a favourite over-indulged pet. 'You are a very, very, wicked young lady.'

Amelia sprung agilely to her feet and turned her attention back to the spellbound Sarah. She undid the final button and then pulled the red coat-dress back off Sarah's shoulders and allowed it to rustle to the floor, where it nestled around Sarah's ankles.

'Oh yes,' Amelia purred appreciatively, almost to herself, her dark eyes working slowly over the sensual contours of Sarah's constrained body. The basque fitted her like a second skin. 'Oh yes... *very* beautiful,' she drooled, licking her lips like a greedy cat with the cream. 'Definitely good enough to eat—'

Before Sarah could do or say anything Amelia matched word to deed. She dropped silently to the floor in front of her and, exactly as she had with Turner, began to nuzzle at the stunned girl's perfumed crotch.

Sarah stiffened in complete shock as Amelia's hair

brushed her thighs, and then she gasped as a wet and skilful tongue lapped majestically across the outer lips of her quim. The sensation was electrifying.

'Oh, my God—' she managed to gasp. Her first inclination was to turn tail and run away, but then she sensed movement behind her. Shooting a glance over her shoulder she saw Casswell, his expression as impassive as ever, but his eyes smouldering with vehement excitement.

He slipped an arm around her waist.

'Open your legs,' he said into her ear, in a tone that brooked no contradiction. 'Let Oliver's pretty little kitten have a taste of the cream.'

Before Sarah could protest he snatched her upper arm fiercely with his free hand and held it painfully tight. As she groaned her dismay he nudged a foot between her feet and prised her legs wide apart. She shrieked as Amelia gripped her hips and dragged her closer, and then plunged her avid tongue into Sarah's sex to trace the engorged ridge of her clitoris.

Sarah closed her eyes, stunned that anything so fleeting could create such an overwhelming wave of pleasure. The tongue flitted and lapped again, making her mewl with pure delight. Was this the magical enchantment that had entrapped Beatrice? Had it been this gift that Beatrice had given, kneeling at her mistress's feet, locked in a passionate embrace so astounding that it overcame all natural revulsion?

Through swirling mists of pleasure Sarah knew Amelia was rapidly taking control, pressing forward, each white-hot kiss driving her out to the very edge of paradise. And as she did Amelia sat back a little and gently guided the handle of the horsewhip up into Sarah's defenceless quim. The delirious captive's head lolled back onto Casswell's shoulder and she whimpered her shock, but did nothing more to protest.

The leather felt obscene and unyielding, and yet her body drew it in gratefully. Casswell tapped her feet wider with his toe, while his hand slipped up from her trim waist to pinch and twisted her erect and throbbing nipples. He lightly kissed her perspiring temple and whispered lewd promises into her ear.

It was all much too much for their besieged victim. As Amelia set the rhythm with her tongue and fingers, and the handle of the whip, Sarah surrendered. She ground down onto the inert black shaft, not caring that she gave the blonde seductress greater access to her restrained body while it drank in the wonderful sensations.

Oliver Turner looked on with evident satisfaction. He rang a discreetly placed bell to summon Chang, who had been waiting for them in an anteroom. When the Oriental appeared he was carrying something in a gloved hand; something that glowed cherry red.

Turner studied Sarah Morgan. The girl was exquisite in the black leather basque, her creamy flesh already shimmering with a fine gloss of perspiration. He knew she was struggling with feelings of revulsion and the more intense call of undiluted, unrestrained passion.

Casswell smiled conspiratorially and held the girl even tighter as Turner moved in. As though forewarned by some strange female intuition, Sarah, on the verge of a shattering orgasm, opened her eyes and saw him too. A strange silence fell over the room as Amelia also glanced up, her full carmine lips slick with Sarah's juices.

Turner smiled; it was a tableau well worth savouring, but it was destined to last no more than a few seconds, although in his mind the whole sensual scene seemed to be played out in slow motion.

Sarah noticed Chang and the object he was holding.

Such prescience. She tried to protest, but all coherent sound was efficiently smothered by Casswell's firm palm. She tried desperately to struggle free, but he was easily too strong and held her with contemptuous ease. With little effort he twisted her in his arms, and as she watched with wide eyes over his fingers, Chang handed the branding iron to Turner, and with a sickening piety, the elderly gentleman sank it onto her exposed right buttock.

Sarah tried to scream into the hand clamped over her mouth, but nothing came up from her lungs. She swooned, felt nauseous, and fell limp and unconscious in Casswell's arms.

Oliver Turner closed his eyes and lifted his face to the high ceiling, luxuriating in the moment.

Chapter Twelve

When Sarah opened her eyes she was quite certain she'd been dreaming. It had been a strange and very intense dream in which her life and Beatrice de Fleur's had finally merged; a peculiar dark fantasy where she had been seduced by another woman – a friend of Oliver Turner's – and then she'd been branded. Something in her mouth, some unfamiliar residue, tasted peculiar too.

She tried to quieten the ramblings of her waking mind and shifted her focus. She was lying on her stomach in an unfamiliar and dimly lit room, on a red moquette couch. As she lifted herself gingerly onto her forearms her head pounded, but she turned very slowly and came face to face with Turner's slave girl, Amelia, sitting elegantly on a chair beside her. She was now wearing a short white cotton robe, which was drawn tightly in at her waist and stretched tautly over her generous breasts. Despite her inner turmoil, Sarah's eyes were drawn inexplicably to the deep shadowy cleavage that nestled within the slightly gaping robe. Amelia laughed musically as she noticed where Sarah's furtive peeps were resting, and leant forward a little to stroke a strand of hair back from the patient's damp brow. The movement only served to open the robe a little more, and Sarah couldn't suppress a soft moan of despair and frustration as the soft perfumed valley hovered even closer.

'Hiya,' Amelia murmured smoothly, the simple greeting just oozing sex. 'Are you okay now? You fainted.'

Sarah swallowed hard, panic and pain suddenly flooding her mind. It hadn't been a dream after all. She could still feel the sensation of the branding iron touching her flesh; a white-hot lightening strike of pain that had unplugged her consciousness. Even now she could feel the remnants of its heat searing into her buttock, a knot of unspeakable rawness that glowed like a neon beacon in her mind. And yet there was also an odd fuzziness to her thinking, and for a second or two Sarah wondered if her thoughts were somehow being muddied by images from Beatrice de Fleur's drugged mind.

Gently, she tried to twist herself around to look at the brand mark, but found it too difficult. All she could see was a thick white surgical dressing, and wondered if it had been Amelia or Chang who had tended to the burn. Her head spun from the effort of trying to crane around, and she closed her eyes to try and clear it.

Amelia touched her arm. 'Don't try and move. Just lie still and rest. Chang gave you something for the pain. It's not very strong, but he said it might make you a bit heady for a little while.'

Sarah closed her eyes tight. The darkness twirled and made her feel sick again. Like a glass marble the centre of the darkness had coloured twists spiralling through it, and the twists in her darkness were pure red pain.

'Why?' she asked at last, opening her eyes. Her mouth and lips were parched.

Amelia smiled and lifted her towelling robe to reveal a tiny brand on her own thigh. No bigger than a man's thumbprint, it was an O overlaid with an ornate T. Sarah had seen the design earlier on the wrought iron gates leading up to the estate, on the front doors to the mansion, and even on the book-plates in the library. It was Oliver Turner's personal mark and Amelia, it seemed, was part of his collection.

Sarah shuddered in dismay; she imagined her own brand to be as big as a saucer, the pain was so great, but guessed that the final scar would probably be just as discreet and imply just as much to anyone who saw it.

'You are marked with the same crest that was used on Beatrice de Fleur,' Casswell said, and Sarah jumped at the sound of his voice, not realising he was with them in the room. 'I thought you would understand and appreciate its significance far more than any other mark we might devise.'

Sarah twisted around, trying to see him.

'Beatrice?' she said, struggling to find her voice. 'How do you know what her brand looked like?'

'It is sketched several times in the original diary. Its design was of great importance to her. I had the iron made up by a local blacksmith.' He was moving closer to Sarah now, and the subtle smell of his cologne made her mouth water. What was this bizarre alchemy?

'Rest now,' he said. 'Chang will be up later to help get you ready for dinner.' He stroked her shoulder, and she shivered under the unexpected caress. 'You did very well today,' he said, leaning so close his breath danced through her silky hair, his voice barely above a whisper. 'I'll see you later.' And then he was gone.

Sarah shook her head again, desperate to clear the remnants of Chang's medicine. Had she detected a strange note of concern in the doctor's voice?

Amelia pulled a soft woollen blanket up around Sarah's shoulders. 'Don't try to fight it, my little darling,' she purred, and just the sound of her soft voice made Sarah's nipples tighten. 'Sleep now. You're going to need all the rest you can get.'

Sarah realised she had no desire or will to resist the invitation. She closed her eyes and let unconsciousness claim her, without really considering the implications of Amelia's last sentence.

'Well, I'm very glad your lovely young lady has suffered no lasting ill-effects from this afternoon's performance,' said Oliver Turner, handing Rigel Casswell a brandy. 'But it is more important that we keep out minds focused on the business in hand. Perhaps I ought to propose a toast for tomorrow. A good luck gesture?'

It was later that evening and, while waiting for dinner to be served, Casswell and Turner were in the study. Casswell was seated comfortably by the roaring fire, reading from the list of guests that Turner had invited to join them to discuss Beatrice's diary.

'And they will all be arriving here tomorrow?'

Turner nodded. 'Indeed they will. Kosford, Lassiter, some chap from Prague who Rees-Miles has recommended. Altogether, it's an impressive gathering. Everyone should be here in time for a breakfast meeting, and by this time tomorrow evening, God willing and a fair wind, we should have all the information we require.'

'And then?' Casswell asked, savouring the sensation of the alcohol as its warmth eased into his bloodstream.

Turner smiled. 'Now, now, my boy. You know that all depends on the combined results of their findings. It's tempting to dream a little though, eh? I have information from a very reliable source that there are several other volumes of Beatrice de Fleur's diaries in existence. Apparently, the collection was kept in the vaults of a monastery near what is now Prague for quite some time. But in the aftermath of the Russian revolution it was broken up for safekeeping. There are supposedly one or two volumes in a museum near Minsk. Another instalment is apparently being kept under lock and key in Berlin. And of course, there are countless stories of other parts of the diaries existing in dusty old libraries and vaults the length and breath of Europe. But then again,' he added philosophically, 'you know how these tales escalate once you express an interest, however discreet the enquiries.' He paused to light a large cigar.

'However, if I get the authentication we need, I might seriously consider sponsoring an expedition to try and track the other volumes down. To the right collector they would be priceless.' Turner lifted his glass in salute to Casswell. 'And it goes without saying that I'll need a man on the ground to protect my interests. At my age I'm really not too keen on undertaking all that fieldwork myself.'

Rigel Casswell smiled with pleasure. It was a commission he would relish. 'In that case, here's to tomorrow, Oliver, and the arrival of the rest of your team of experts.'

The dancing fire reflected in Turner's eyes as he gently tapped his glass against Casswell's. 'Indeed, dear boy. And here's to the endless search for new pleasures, and the marking of your precious little slave girl.'

Casswell laughed and returned the gesture. The chinking of the crystal glasses echoed around the elegant room. 'Talking of slave girls, Amelia looks very well these days, Oliver. Your new attraction in the museum had me completely fooled.'

The elderly gentleman preened with delight. 'Oh yes,

quite excellent isn't it? She's a wonderful girl, but she really does need to be kept in line. Like Sarah, she is high-spirited and needs a firm hand. I have to ensure that she's reminded regularly exactly who is the master in this house, and who the slave. Which, of course, is exactly how it should be. I want impassioned obedience, a challenge, a lively companion with a little fire in their loins, not some snivelling little mouse.'

'As ever,' smiled Casswell, 'I agree with you wholeheartedly.'

They glanced across the room to where Amelia was tied. Spread-eagled and naked except for her long leather boots and the broad, studded belt fastened tight around her waist, the slim blonde awaited the men's pleasure.

'Why don't you help yourself?' offered Turner, with a nod of his head. 'Let me see how my favourite apprentice fares these days.'

Casswell smiled thinly, accepted the generous gesture with a curt bow from the waist, and picked up a short flexible whip from amongst the wide selection on offer on the sideboard. Whilst Sarah Morgan slept off the effects of Chang's sleeping potion and recovered a little from her branding, he would be only too pleased to take his host up on his kind offer of hospitality. He knew he needed to satisfy the little plume of passion that lay like a coiled snake in his belly.

He flexed the whip speculatively. He could see Amelia was already trembling, and wondered how long it had been since she'd had a proper beating. Oliver Turner was robust for his age, but the years had not been overly kind to his mentor. He doubted whether the older man had much stamina these days – and Amelia liked it rough.

He saw her tense as he approached, and then she

relaxed, probably assuming he would have a practice stroke or two before laying on the punishment in earnest.

How wrong she was.

Casswell swept the tasselled end of the whip back and brought it down with a resounding crack across her creamy back. He watched her struggle to snatch a breath, and then a split second later she shrieked like a banshee, her body thrashing into a wild spasm of pain, breasts thrusting forward, legs splayed wide as she struggled instinctively to escape the cruel kiss of the leather.

'You *bastard*, Rigel!' she hissed with gritted teeth as he swung the whip again. Casswell and Amelia went back a long way.

The whip cracked again and again, with no more than seconds between the strokes. It was relentless. If the luscious blonde had any further curses to expel they were lost in a high-pitched mewl of pain.

Sarah kept catching glimpses of her reflection on the way down to one of the living rooms. A mirror here, a glass door there – and she was totally entranced by what she saw. Chang's innate ability to emphasise the beauty of the female form was really quite astonishing. She glanced at him; he was a true paradox, swinging between willing and gentle servant, and something far less benign.

Tonight, she was wearing a strapless black velvet evening dress, lightly boned to emphasis her full breasts and narrow waist. Beneath it she was again wearing the basque and stockings she had arrived in – one outfit complementing the other perfectly. Chang had added long black silk gloves, and around her throat her only ornament was a diamanté collar. The overall effect was perfection.

Chang had led her down through the house from the bedroom where she had slept off the effects of his painkilling potion. He walked a pace or two ahead of her, in total silence, a solicitous guide, opening doors, directing her through the quietly understated luxury of Oliver Turner's enormous country mansion.

Despite his silence, or perhaps because of it, Sarah felt more uncertain in his company tonight than usual, although there was nothing noticeably different that she could put her finger on. While dressing her he had been as efficient as ever; but there was something indefinable and disturbing about his demeanour that unnerved her. It was as though he knew some dark secret to which she was not to be privy.

To allay her fears she tried to concentrate on her surroundings. Turner's house was a stunning contrast to Doctor Casswell's run-down gothic pile; plush carpets, exquisite antique furniture, glittering chandeliers.

At the door to the living room Chang paused and indicated for her to enter. She hesitated. She could hear indistinct sounds from within that unsettled her, and as she lifted a knuckle to knock on the polished oak, the evening was shaken by the sound of something swiping viciously through the air and an impassioned scream.

An icy chill stabbed down Sarah's spine and her flesh crawled. She knew it was Amelia Cartwright. She knew she was being beaten; being beaten by Doctor Rigel Casswell. She froze, her gloved hand over her mouth.

'Go on in,' Chang coaxed.

Sarah couldn't bear to witness the possible horrors on the other side of the door, but something compelling drew her like a magnet. Her hand dropped slowly to the handle, she pressed down, the door creaked a little, and she drifted hypnotically into the room. So mesmerised was she by the tableaux before her that she didn't really hear Chang quietly close the door and leave her in the company of Casswell and the sobbing slave.

In the middle of the room Amelia hung in a purpose-built wooden frame, rivulets of sweat running down between her shoulder-blades. Her skin was pale, while across her back were at least a dozen scarlet weals that served to accentuate the creaminess of her supple body.

Casswell stood behind her, legs akimbo, cradling a whip. His eyes were feverish with gratification as he stared salaciously at the timid newcomer.

'Well, how very nice of you to join us, Miss Morgan,' he said with a throaty growl. 'And how very delicious you look this evening, I must say. I'm certain Amelia would appreciate a little feminine tenderness and solace. Perhaps you would like to return the compliment she paid you earlier; a little cream for my kitten?'

Sarah reddened, but found herself drawn towards the naked slave, despite the strong desire to turn and run from the oppressive room. She realised, to her utter dismay, that part of her was jealous of the female and the sadistic attention Casswell was lavishing on her. She swallowed hard and shook her head, trying to dispel the incredible yearning.

Tiny beads of sweat glistened on Casswell's top lip. 'Come along, my dear,' he snapped as Sarah reached the frame. 'Do not keep me waiting.'

Without thinking, Sarah reached out and ran a gloved finger over Amelia's naked shoulder. Amelia groaned softly. Sarah could smell the other woman's body. It was a strange heady perfume; a mixture of eau de cologne, and darker, more oceanic scents.

Casswell's expression hardened. Sarah knew exactly what he expected, and she knew that, no matter how much the prospect appalled her, she wouldn't deny him. Without a word, despite the smart of the brand still hurting her flesh, Sarah sank to her knees in front of Amelia and pressed a single kiss to the trussed blonde's flat belly.

Amelia gasped.

Sarah shivered and then lowered her head; a supplicant at the ancient altar of desire. And in that instant, as she ran her tongue along the naked junction of Amelia's fragrant sex, she understood a little of what arcane magic drew men to this sacred place.

The delicate skin beneath her lips was warm, moist and salty, and trembled in the aftermath of pain and fear. It was as soft as spun silk and as fragrant as new mown hay. Any revulsion was tempered with a strange sense of resignation and wanting.

Amelia, her kohl-streaked eyes dark with need and blurred with tears, gazed down at her. 'Please, Sarah,' she whispered hoarsely, 'take the pain away, set me free, I need the antidote... take me to the edge.'

Sarah shivered again; there was no going back. As her tongue parted the lips of Amelia's quim her senses were totally overwhelmed. The act of worship was as old as time itself and beyond any rational explanation. All she could taste was the salty gossamer of Amelia's excitement. All she could smell was the rich perfume of Amelia's pleasure.

Casswell smiled as he watched Sarah open Amelia's quim with her gloved fingers and then press her face forward. Her eyes were closed and her tentative tongue circled and stroked back and forth across the swollen bud that nestled between those engorged lips, and then her mouth settled on Amelia's flesh.

It was such a beautiful sight to see: the naked and bound beauty, her stretched body still perspiring and marked from the kiss of the whip, and the subservient Sarah on her hands and knees, in full evening dress, her head buried between the other's thighs, and her tongue paying homage to those wet and fragrant folds.

'Shall we join the adorable ladies, my boy?' said a voice at his shoulder. Such was the tension in the room, Oliver Turner had been able to slip in unnoticed.

'Why not,' Casswell said, with a sly grin at his friend and mentor.

Turner nodded towards the frame. 'Any particular preference?'

Casswell shook his head. It crossed his mind that it was almost a shame to disturb the lovely twosome.

But Turner wanted his share of the fun.

He sidled up behind his beautiful willowy blonde and ran his hands up over her ribs to cup her breasts. His lips brushed the curve of her neck and her shoulders, while thick fingers toyed with her nipple rings. With her eyes tightly closed, Amelia moaned and wriggled seductively against her master; an invitation so unmistakable it made the watching Casswell's penis lurch in his trousers. From the tension in her muscles and her staccato breathing he knew she was already careering towards a mighty orgasm. The elderly gentleman fumbled with his trousers and unleashed his straining member. Without hesitation he thrust his hips forward and entered Amelia with one accurate lunge.

Crouched between the blonde's legs Sarah was completely entranced, eyes closed, she was making soft slurping noises of pleasure as she nuzzled, lapped and fingered Amelia's throbbing quim. As Casswell watched, Turner's gnarled erection slipped between those rich moist folds. Sarah obediently lapped at the underside of that too, as it speared up into the blonde's waiting body.

Casswell noticed she'd slipped a hand down between her own legs. Just like Beatrice de Fleur, Sarah was seeking her own pleasure, longing to travel the same road as the luscious slave who gyrated and moaned above her.

He dropped to his knees behind Sarah, suddenly desperate to be a part of the end game, and lifted the soft velvet folds of her skirt. She dipped her back and ground her hips towards him. Under the lightest of caresses her juicy sex opened like an exotic flower. Casswell smiled; his slave was everything he had ever hoped for – and more. Unfastening his fly he pressed his curved shaft home without any further prelude. She reached back between her parted thighs and her silken fingers joined his, guiding and welcoming his phallus home.

She needed him as much as he wanted her.

Sarah's body enfolded him, drawing him deep, deep into the ocean of delights. Above them, Amelia suddenly cried out with pleasure and began to thrust raggedly back and forth against Sarah's busy tongue. Casswell groaned and bit down on Sarah's shoulder, making her whimper with pain and thrust back onto him all the harder.

Within seconds all four of them were lost amongst the crashing white-plumed waves of pleasure. The moment of climax echoed and re-echoed through them all; a continuous charge, so intense it was impossible to decipher where one person's pleasure began and another's ended.

An hour later dinner was being served by Turner's uniformed staff in an elegant room overlooking the gardens and the ornamental lake. The table glittered with a wealth of silver, cut crystal and crisp white linen. Sarah took a genteel sip of her soup and glanced surreptitiously around the table.

In the candlelight the setting looked so opulent. At the head of the table Oliver Turner looked like an elder statesman, a successful mature businessman at ease, while seated beside him Amelia could easily be taken for his niece or goddaughter. The blonde was now dressed in a stunning copper silk column dress that whispered wealth and emphasised her exquisite creamy skin. With her hair dressed and her make-up applied to perfection she looked for all the world as though she had spent the evening making polite chit-chat and passing around appetising hors-d'oeuvres. Further down the table their guests – a distinguished-looking academic in a beautifully cut dinner-jacket and his companion, wife, lover, it would be hard to tell which – sat in companionable silence while their host told them about his recent trip to North Africa.

Sarah doubted that anyone would ever guess the true nature of the liaison.

She could still feel the silky juices of excitement trickling and pooling in the warm space between her thighs; the good Doctor Casswell's excitement mingling with hers. In sharp contrast, every time she moved she was reminded of the raw stab of the branding iron. Pleasure and pain, was there ever a more heady cocktail?

'A little more wine, my dear?' asked Casswell politely, indicating her glass.

Sarah nodded. The food was superb, and the conversation between Casswell, Turner and Amelia flowed seamlessly and merrily between art and music and history, on past the theatre and recent exhibitions; matters Sarah knew very little about.

As if he sensed her feelings of isolation Casswell stroked her cheek; it was the gesture both of reassurance and possession. 'Your education is only just beginning,' he murmured in a low voice. Sarah nodded and blushed under what she sensed was his growing approval.

Chapter Thirteen

In the conference room the following morning Rigel Casswell refilled his coffee cup and then glanced down at the typed notes he had been given by Oliver. The long narrow room had formerly been a covered walkway, and its large arched windows gave a breathtaking view out over the rolling parkland of Oliver's country estate. Its shape concentrated the attention firmly on a low and subtly lit dais backed by a screen. Casswell stretched – it promised to be a fine day. Already the mist was lifting off the lake, softening the shards of the morning sunshine. He added a splash of milk to the coffee and went to find his seat.

The room was busy with the low murmuring of in-depth conversations. Gathered around the large oval table were some of the world's foremost experts on historical erotic literature.

On the dais, standing behind a clear lectern, Rupert Lassiter, the first of the day's speakers, re-lit his pipe, quickly called his audience to order, and then began his discourse. His role had been to confirm and verify the existence of Beatrice's diary from other written sources of the time. He spoke with bluff good humour about letters between bishops commending the care of the work to the other, and a letter from two honoured guests who had been privileged enough to see the diaries on a visit to the religious order and had written – very discreetly – to thank the Abbot for his kindness in letting them read extracts from it. And then, to peals of laughter from the gathered men and women, he added that the guests went on to praise the Abbot for the two ripe serving wenches he had lent them to take away 'the powerful ache for pleasures of the flesh that lingered in the aftermath of reading the Mistress de Fleur's astonishing journal'.

'Here,' said Lassiter, pointing with the stem of his pipe to a screen behind him, 'are some very nice photographic reproductions of the lists of contents of the chests that rested in the Abbey. And here, a complete inventory of the holy and secular books stored in the Abbot's private library at the turn of the last century. Rather like an inner sanctum it was here that the order's treasures where kept, both for safekeeping and as, with these diaries, to keep them from prying uneducated eyes. And here—' he tapped some lines of faint, almost indecipherable hand-written text, '—we appear to have a record of the complete work that interests us. As you will see, the diaries were listed in the centre of the page, their titles amongst a column of several other volumes. That's a very good sign. I would have been far less happy had these appeared at the foot or head of the page, as this could infer tampering. And by that I mean that the works had been added to the inventory at a later date. Now if we move on to contemporaneous accounts of—'

A hand went up on the far side of the table. A delegate from America began to speak in a lazy mid-western drawl. 'I would like to make this point clear, Doctor Lassiter. Are we saying there is definitely more than one volume?'

Lassiter nodded. 'Oh, absolutely, it would certainly appear so, yes. All the documentary evidence points to there being several small books, all very much like the one Oliver has in his possession. Small, portable, quite crudely made by Beatrice or one of her compatriots. But yes, four, perhaps more volumes. A very rare thing indeed, I grant you, but for us quite a miraculous find.'

There was a murmur of surprise and pleasure around the table, while Rupert Lassiter turned his attention back to his notes. 'Now, as I was saying, next I moved on to the contemporaneous accounts of...'

But Casswell's thinking had already moved on, to thoughts of Sarah and Amelia making love to each other in Oliver's private apartments while he looked on. He imagined the two girls dressed as a matched pair, in black shiny leather, a studded collar around each of their necks and a matching body harness that lifted their breasts and then, after circling their slim waists, framed each thigh so that their sex was naked and exposed. He shivered at the delightful image. He would order Sarah to tie Amelia into the frame they had used the night before and then beat her with a rigid leather paddle he had with him. He swallowed hard, imagining the sound as it bit into the blonde's succulent flesh.

He had seen the compassion in Sarah's eyes when she had discovered Amelia hanging from the frame. How very hard it would be for her to overcome her fear and reluctance, to obey his orders and lay on with the strap. Or perhaps it would be better if it was the other way around. In his mind he reversed their roles, imagining Sarah now writhing with pure delight as Amelia abandoned the paddle and fell to her knees, driving her tongue deep into the secret places on Sarah's tied and sweating body. She would be caught on Amelia's wriggling tongue like a beautiful bird in a trap, writhing and sobbing as the pulse of orgasm throbbed through her. Oh yes, that would be delightful. Casswell closed his eyes and let the fantasy take flight.

Upstairs, well away from the conference, Sarah woke to find herself naked and alone in a vast double bed in one of the guestrooms. She stretched a little and rubbed the sleep from her eyes, while piecing together the events of the previous evening. Her fingers strayed to her throat and touched the collar and chain that was fast becoming part of her bedtime ritual.

After a very civilised dinner she and Amelia had kept Turner and Casswell company in the billiard room until quite late, and then... she sighed at the memory.

As the night had drawn on the conversation moved to a project that Turner had been involved in, in central Europe. It had been a long and involved story about the stultifying effects of a cumbersome and inefficient bureaucracy. As the tale unfolded Turner's voice had dropped to a low hypnotic murmur, and Sarah found it impossible to keep her eyes open. She remembered with some embarrassment the creeping feeling of tiredness she seemed powerless to resist.

The combination of a superb dinner, the wine, and her unexpected encounter with Amelia, began to take effect – or perhaps it was Chang's painkilling potion. Whatever, when Doctor Casswell had suggested she retire for the night she had been deeply grateful. Chang had brought her up to this room.

For a little while after she undressed she had waited in the velvety darkness, fighting the call of sleep, wondering if Amelia or Rigel Casswell, or perhaps even Oliver Turner, might come and slip into her bed under the cover of night. But as the minutes ticked by her grip on consciousness gradually loosened.

For the first time in many nights her sleep had been blessedly dreamless.

Now morning sunlight pushed its way between the closed curtains. Sarah stretched again. Her body ached and as her back and thigh muscles contracted she was vividly reminded of the brand. She winced, and then heard a noise from close by. In an alcove by the door Chang was hanging the dress she had worn the night before onto a padded hanger.

She was quite surprised to see him there; assuming that he would be attending to the doctor. He looked up as she moved.

'It is late, high time you were up,' he said, without emotion.

Sarah glanced at the bedside clock – it was after ten. Hastily she began to scramble off the bed, wondering why he hadn't called her before. What would Doctor Casswell say if she turned up late?

Chang swung round. 'But there is no need for you to hurry this morning. The doctor will not be wanting you until later in the day, although he has left you some work to be getting on with.' He nodded towards the desk where, to Sarah's surprise, lay the loose-leaf folder containing the transcript of Beatrice's diary, and beside it the familiar bulk of a computer like the one in Doctor Casswell's study. 'Would you like me to ring for some breakfast?'

She nodded, wondering why the doctor hadn't mentioned the arrangements earlier, but she knew Chang would be angry if she spoke without being spoken too. Did that mean that from now on she could only speak when he asked her a direct question?

He grinned, the expression quite uncanny on his

normally impassive face. 'So, Sarah Morgan, it would appear that once your chores are done for today you are mine and Oscar's... you remember Oscar, Mr Turner's chauffeur?'

Sarah didn't moved. She remembered her encounter with Oscar only to well. Images of the heavy silver ring that pierced his foreskin flashed unbidden through her consciousness, and for some reason she wondered if it was the same design as the rings Amelia wore through her nipples.

Chang's expression hardened alarmingly. 'I asked you a question, girl,' he growled. Sarah struggled to find her voice, but before she could reply he reached across the bed and slapped her face.

'Do you remember him now?' he repeated. He caught hold of the chain around her neck and wound it around his fist, pulling her closer.

Sarah nodded. The blow was so unexpected that her eyes filled with tears of surprise and pain. She wondered why he thought it necessary to be so brutal. He must surely realise she was in no position to refuse him whatever it was he wanted. 'Yes,' she whispered sulkily, as she rubbed her tingling cheek. 'Yes, I do remember him.'

Chang nodded. 'That's better.' His eyes worked down over her nakedness, taking in her stiffening nipples and the tempting fullness of her breasts.

Sarah tensed under his cool appraisal.

'Several of the other guests have brought their girls here with them,' he continued. His smile broadened a little. 'Or their boys, whichever takes their fancy. What is certain is that after today's meeting the masters and their slaves will be invited to join Mr Turner in the

drawing room for one of his special little get-togethers.'
He stroked the reddening blotch on her cheek. She
shivered; there was no comfort in his touch. 'I'm sure
you'll love it. They usually hold a charity auction after
dinner to raise a little money for their own pet causes.'

Sarah stared at him, aware that this apparently innocent
piece of information intimated far more. Chang stroked
his hand back across her cheek, then down to her breasts,
and rolled one pert nipple between thumb and forefinger,
making her flinch as he nipped it spitefully. 'Do you
want to know what it is they intend to auction?'

Sarah took a deep breath. She could already guess
what they intended to auction.

Arranging himself beside her on the bed, Chang
continued, 'Your sweet little body, that's what. Your
sweet little body and the body of every other slave in the
house. The good doctor will sell you off to the highest
bidder for the night, or just for a damned good beating.
Or perhaps to take part in the floor show.' The little
Oriental's dark eyes were glinting excitedly. 'You know
of course that when Doctor Casswell finally tires of you
he will bring you to a place like this. He will bring you
to Mr Turner's, or one of the other connoisseurs on the
circuit, and sell you like so much horse flesh.' He paused
for effect. Sarah tried hard not to let the shock register
on her face.

'Or sometimes,' Chang continued, his eyes not leaving
hers as his fingers continued their brazen exploration of
her breasts, 'there is no money involved, and a slave is
handed on like a bitch or dog that's fallen from favour.'

Sarah could smell the man's growing heat, and feel
the slightest tremor in his fingers. She knew he was
talking himself into a state of arousal. She wondered

what remembered images from auctions past lurked behind those beady eyes. She was determined not to show her fear of him, but it was difficult. She knew he hoped intimidation would make her more compliant.

With the sound of her pulse pounding in her ears, she said slowly, 'So is that how Doctor Casswell got you?'

To her surprise Chang laughed, and then grabbed her shoulders and jerked her close to him, so his face was mere inches from hers and her traitorously erect nipples brushed the front on his coarse blue shirt.

'Be very careful how far you push me, Sarah Morgan. I've told you before that you really do need me on your side. You would do well not to forget that very important lesson. Life with Doctor Casswell will be far easier for you if I am your friend.'

Sarah refused to look away and bravely held his aggressive stare, even though she knew she was being provocative.

Chang grinned. It made him look like a shark. Before Sarah could respond defensively he grasped the back of her neck and kissed her fiercely. His tongue twisted like a worm and forced itself deep into her mouth. She pushed against his chest, and then he spitefully bit her lower lip. Sarah squealed at the shock and pain as he quickly pulled away and pushed her face down towards his groin. At the same time he snatched her wrist in a vicelike grip and pressed her palm into his crotch. She could feel his erection through the fabric of his sweat pants and instinctively tried to resist the pressure of his fingers. Chang laughed again, but without a shred of humour.

'Oh, very good,' he panted, 'very good indeed. You know, I enjoy it even more if you resist me, Sarah. Don't you understand that? Today you are mine to do with

163

exactly as I please. The doctor will be busy all day. You had better not forget that.'

Sarah made one last attempt to twist away from his grasp but he was far too strong for her. She had little choice but to do as he demanded. He tugged down the waistband of his trousers with one hand and his raging cock sprang free and speared up before her wide eyes. The purple head was swollen and smooth, and already glistened with the slick juices of his excitement.

'You know exactly what I want,' Chang hissed between clenched teeth, 'so don't play silly games with me.'

The raw smell of his masculinity made her tremble as he jerked his hips towards her vulnerable face. She reluctantly caught his rigid column between her fingers, and cupped his distended testicles. She knew it wouldn't be enough to satisfy him; he wanted her to fellate him, and nothing less would do.

It was pointless to try and fight. She closed her eyes and steeled herself, and then drew his cock between her lips. She ran her tongue around the sensitive foreskin where it surrounded and rolled back from the engorged crown. As she pressed the very tip of her tongue into the single eye, Chang sighed and lay back amongst the tangle of sheets, his hand still resting on the back of her neck in case she was foolish enough to do anything silly.

'That's better,' he mumbled. 'That's much, much better.'

Crouched between his legs she could feel his dominance. Everything about Chang's body language and demeanour was designed to assert that here in the shadows of this bedroom, far away from the protection of Doctor Casswell and Oliver Turner, he was the master and she the slave.

She shuffled into a more comfortable kneeling position between his spread thighs, finally relinquishing the fight in her belly. With her tongue and fingers and artful mouth working in harmony she gave him what he wanted; a simple act of complete surrender. But what perturbed her most was that amongst her sense of anger and humiliation, she could also feel the first flickers of excitement.

Sarah closed her eyes, angry with herself, trying to suppress her need. With each lapping stroke she brought Chang closer and closer to his climax, and fought to hold back her own growing need. There would be time enough later to caress and stroke herself to that sweet point of no return, when Chang was gone and she was alone.

At last she felt Chang's muscles tense under her fingertips, and heard his panting quicken. Sarah steeled herself in readiness of his ejaculation. But at the very last second he jerked his cock out from between her lips and, as he grunted like a pig, a warm tidal wave of semen splashed across her breasts and chin, the clammy seed clinging to her glowing skin.

Sarah recoiled in frustration and surprise and looked up at him. His eyes glinted like jet. He wiped himself and then lay back for a few seconds, his gaze locked to hers, silently denying her the right to clean herself. Her heart thumped a frantic rhythm in her chest, and she wondered what would follow. He grinned slyly, and then rolled over and took something from the bedside drawer.

'Here,' he said with a lecherous leer, 'I've brought you a little something from Mr Turner's precious collection downstairs. I thought you might enjoy a little company, seeing as I won't be able to satisfy you for a while yet.' His eyes flickered down to the pearly emission coating her throat and breasts, to emphasise his meaning. Sarah glanced surreptitiously at his flaccid penis lying shrivelled and glistening over the waistband of his trousers, confirming his satiated condition.

Sarah gasped. In his hand, Chang cradled a thick and exquisitely modelled phallus, set along its length with a multitude of small smooth sparkling precious looking stones. He pressed it firmly between her breasts, and rolled it lewdly back and forth in his own semen.

'Lay back and open your legs,' he ordered flatly.

Sarah stared at him in disgust, but knew it was pointless to deny him. He would get what he wanted, one way or another. He took her fingers and wrapped them around the inert phallus, pushed her lifeless thighs apart, and guided it between them. She closed her eyes and shuddered as the thing rubbed over her flesh. It was made of something slightly flexible and warm to the touch. She sighed with shame as it brushed lightly and crept up her inner thighs towards its target; her sex was already wet, the inner lips slick with the juices of her growing excitement – the excitement that only seconds before was her own wicked secret.

Chang spread her legs wider still and gently pressed the end of the dildo into the moist void. To Sarah's chagrin she opened willingly like the petals of a flower, before closing hungrily around the uneven shaft and drawing it into the reaches of her body.

Her tormentor sat back on his haunches. 'Now touch yourself,' he encouraged, his voice thick with his returning excitement. He guided her wet fingers to her engorged clitoris. 'Don't tell me that you don't want to. I can feel how excited you are, Sarah. Casswell was right about you – you really are a natural. Now touch yourself. I want to watch you come.' As he mesmerised her befuddled mind with his dulcet tones he began to ease the thick black phallus back and forth, in and out, encouraging Sarah to do the same of her own accord.

She nibbled her lip and closed her eyes tight, her sense of humiliation complete. While modesty demanded she fight him off and roll away, her body demanded release. Her finger circled the hardened ridge of her clitoris, sending pure pleasure soaring through her. She was stunned by just how responsive her body was. Hopelessly lost, and no longer caring about the presence of the man who squatted and leered down at the writhing feast before him, she began to pump the dildo. Her fingers worked eagerly back and forth across her pleasure bud, until she knew there was no going back – she knew she was plunging towards an explosive orgasm.

Rolling her head from side to side and whimpering incoherently, Sarah arched her back and instinctively thrust up onto the carved phallus.

'Look at me,' Chang whispered in her ear. 'Look at me.'

Her eyes opened, and she knew he was toying with her like a cat toys with a mouse. As the first fires of orgasm roared through her she realised that his pleasure was intensifying the sensations she was feeling. Wave after wave engulfed her, but above it all she could see Chang's dark eyes fixed on hers, drinking in every nuance, every tremor, every ripple of her joy.

Ten minutes later Sarah stood in the shower and let the refreshing water cascade down over her body, washing away the last remnants of Chang's passion. She was still trembling and realised, as she turned her face up to the torrent, that she had begun to live her life day to day, hour to hour, minute to minute, with no thought for the future, no longer looking ahead. Her whole life revolved around Doctor Casswell and his plans for her.

She reached up and let the water play over her back, only too aware of the sensation the torrent lit on the skin still raw from the brand. Chang – returned to his role of nursemaid and jailer once his passion was sated – had said he would dress it when he returned.

Closing her eyes she contemplated Chang's comments regarding Oliver Turner's guests, their slaves, the party, and the auction. She wondered if it was the truth, or just part of some dark fantasy he'd been spinning to persuade her into submission. It was a strange and compelling game they were playing.

Taking a towel from the warmed rail she dried herself. In the bedroom, on the desk, were the computer and the loose-leaf folder, and she was drawn to it once again. It would a relief to step back into Beatrice de Fleur's world for a while. Wrapping the towel around her she opened the book to the marked page and sat down to read. It took no more than seconds for her to become oblivious to her wet hair and the stinging sensation of rough towelling again the burn.

Chapter Fourteen

...I awoke to find myself lying on a large curtained bed, with my hands tied above my head. The rope was slack, enabling me to turn a little. Although naked, my flesh burnt with an unnatural heat and I felt sick and dizzy. On my backside the fresh sore from the branding iron made me want to weep, but I kept my peace; I was not alone. Out beyond the ornate drapes I could see torches glowing in the wall sconces and from close by I could hear the low murmur of voices.

Although my head and my body ached most pitifully I thanked all the saints that whatever noxious potion my lady had poured down my throat it had not finished me off completely – although I could still feel its effects in my blood.

As my head cleared a little I listened more closely to the conversation, and after a moment or two I realised it was her ladyship and that blaggard Arturo. What they were discussing made my blood run ice cold.

'You worry too much, madam. The deed will be carried out down by the river as we have already arranged,' said Arturo, with an edge to his voice as if he explained this plan to her many, many times before.

My lady made noises of approval, and I heard the sound of wine or something similar being poured into two vessels. 'Please forgive me, Arturo. I know you think me foolish, but this is of the greatest importance. We cannot afford to fail now, not this close to our goal. I have to be certain these assassins you have hired will do the job. My husband, for all his faults, is a most popular man. Are you certain they will be able to carry out what is required of them when the time comes?'

Arturo groaned. 'Murder, my lady. That is the word you fight so shy of. Of course they will. These men are hired mercenaries. How many times do I have to assure you of their loyalty to you and to the mother church? They are hired from the house of Carun, who are the sworn enemies of your husband. They and their families have been brought to the very edge of ruin by the taxes he has levied upon their estates. Trust me, lady, they will be only too happy to dispatch your husband to his maker. And if there was any doubt lingering, the purse of gold I pressed into their greedy paws convinced them of the justness of our cause.'

'And they are here now? They are in the castle?'

'They came in just before curfew, disguised as merchants, and are even sleeping now under the shelter of the castle walls. They will be in their place by cock-crow tomorrow. Have no fear your ladyship, it is all arranged. Your husband, the Lord Usher, and I, are to leave for the hunt by first light, and as we pass through the stand of trees down by the ford the ambush will be sprung. A swift blow from a well placed sword blade and your husband and his feckless cousin will be no more.'

There was a moment or two's silence, and then my ladyship said, 'Good, 'tis just a shame that that dissolute priest will not to be amongst the hunting party. Once my husband is dead I want you to eliminate that evil old man with all haste. He chills me to the very marrow. Had it not been for him I believe my father would never

170

have married me off in the first place.' There was another pause and then she added, 'And what of your little trollop, Arturo? For all your words in the heat of passion and the maw of lust are you sure you want her with you? Are you sure you can master her? Would it not be better to turn her loose now while she can be of no trouble to either of us? There are whores a-plenty all over the city that will do exactly as you bid them for a handful of coppers, and who have no history that might condemn us.'

Arturo laughed. 'I am certain of it, my lady. I would have her with me, truly.'

As if forewarned by some other sense, I lay stock still on the bed and closed my eyes. A second or two later Arturo drew aside the curtains that draped my fetid cell. From behind half-closed lids I watched him gaze down upon me, examining my nakedness with an unhealthy interest. I sensed that some part of him wanted me because I belonged to the man who, for some reason, he perceived to be his enemy. In his mind I was little more than his master's toy and he, a peasant, wanted nothing more than to have me for his own, to prove he was as good as the man he planned to betray and murder.

'Have no fear, my lady,' he said, running his hateful hands up over my thighs and stroking a finger up into the tight reaches of my quim. 'I will master her. And when all this is over and settled, I think I shall take her as my wife. Always at my beck and call, my bed companion. And I shall keep her like this, naked and tied until she is fully broken.' He cupped my belly and stroked it thoughtfully. 'I would like her to bear me sons.' Feigning sleep, I moaned softly and turned a little under his touch so as not to arouse his suspicions, while my mind raced with fear and hatred.

His despicable finger sank a little deeper and I moved against it sleepily, as if all that was left in my drugged frame was the force that drives an animal to couple with its mate; not reason, not sound-thinking, but only the thrust of nature and the heat of the rut.

Arturo seemed much pleased with my response.

'What is it that holds you there? Does she stir? Do you think she's heard what we said?' asked my lady anxiously. 'If that is the case we may need to rethink her fate. Is she awake?'

Arturo cupped one breast, his fingers working at the nipple until it hardened under his insistent caress. 'No, not yet, lady. Look, she sleeps like a babe. The draught you gave her works still, but not enough so she loses all feelings. Look how she moves so freely against me. Perhaps...' I could hear the amusement and suppressed excitement in his voice, '... perhaps we might have a little more fun with her while she rests.'

Her ladyship snorted. 'Don't be so ridiculous, man. We need her to stay asleep. Sometimes Arturo, I think your entire life is governed by that great thing that hangs between your legs. I have already explained, I must go downstairs and entertain that buffoon Usher so no one is suspicious of my absence. I am late already. Is your whore well tied?'

Arturo, fooled by my sleepiness and perhaps still thinking about my feigned compliance, gave the rope the most superficial of inspections.

'Aye. She is secure.'

'Good,' said my lady. 'Leave her there, then. Best you gag her too so she won't be able to attract anyone's attention if she does happen to wake.'

Arturo did as he was asked, and I struggled not to retch as he thrust a filthy rag into my mouth and bound it tight with another – all the time aware that I was supposed to be in a drugged stupor.

'Hurry up,' snapped my ladyship. 'Time is racing.'

I suspect Arturo's progress was greatly hampered by the fact that he could hardly bear to leave me thus: naked, tied and alone and unable to resist his advances. It was everything he could have possibly wanted and more. His fingers frantically travelled feverishly between my breasts and my sex. For two pins I knew he would have stayed.

Finally my lady appeared behind him, her face contorted with anger. 'For God's sake leave her be, man. There will be time enough for your questionable pleasures later. If we are not down in the hall soon our absence will arouse all manner of trouble.'

And so finally, after what seemed like an eternity, I was alone. With the door closed fast I slipped off the ropes that bound me and spat out the evil rag that silenced me. I had to find a way to warn my master – and quickly. I scrambled off the bed, fighting the nausea and the dizziness that threatened to undo me. Still naked, I hurried to the great oak door, my head spinning from the after-effects of my ladyship's noxious potion.

It seems the saints were on my side that night, for I was just about to throw open the door when I heard muffled voices coming from outside. Crouching on my hands and knees I peered through the keyhole into the passageway beyond. Lolling idly against the wall were two of the household guards, no doubt set there by Arturo to keep watch.

Although my brain was still addled, I held back for a

moment or two. I had no idea what instructions the men had been given. Would they let me by without reporting what they had seen? Unlikely. My master's life was at risk. I had to warn him, and dare not take the chance of discovery. Perhaps I might pass by as my lady's maid, left behind in her chambers to tidy. But not naked, as I was now.

Hastily I looked around the room for something suitable to wear. Discarded on the settle a fine white linen petticoat – a beginning at least. I pulled it on, and as I did I saw by one of the great tapestries on the wall, almost concealed by an ornamental wooden pier, was a narrow door set back into the stonework.

I had heard many tales that the castle was riddled with secret passages, and wondered if this was one such passage. Picking up a blanket for a cloak, I wound it around my shoulders and then eased open the concealed door. The cold air hit me like a rush of water. Sure enough, out beyond the door was a little landing and a narrow spiral staircase that wound down into the gloom. Afraid I would lose heart if I delayed too long, I plucked a torch from a wall sconce and warily began my descent into the inky darkness.

In my drugged state it seemed a strange and almost unreal journey that appeared to twist down into the very bowels of the earth. I had to keep tight hold of my thoughts to stop them from running away with sheer terror. At each landing – and there were many – I listened through the doors that presented themselves and looked where I could, to see if I might find safe passage back to my master's apartments, or even to the chapel to find Father Orme. Several of the doors were locked from the inside, and those that weren't were in parts of the castle that were unfamiliar to me. I was too afraid to risk getting lost. Finally, after what seemed like an age, I realised I had reached the ground floor and the courtyard, and with a great rush of relief I pushed open a heavy wooden door that led outside.

The smell of the night air filled my senses. A brazier burned brightly in the lee of a wall, and as my eyes adjusted to the gloom I saw I was not alone. At first I thought I was surrounded by simple travelling peasant folk who had come in to the castle for the night to take shelter from the dangers of the open road.

And then my heart sank.

Staring at me with a mixture of surprise and disbelief were a group of four or five people. They were working men and they had been drinking. I looked across towards the night watchman's station. It seemed an awful long way, and I knew my bare feet, the rough blanket, and the thin wisp of a petticoat were scant protection against the chill night air – or anything else.

One man, eyes bright with beer and lust, stepped forward, and pushing the door closed behind me, trapped me between his arms. He leered down. His breath was foul.

'Why, hello my pretty thing. What brings you out on a night like this, so poorly dressed against the cold? Seems to me you're in need of a good man who can warm you through and keep you a-bed nights.'

He laughed and tugged at my blanket as he spoke. Had he been sober I would have called on his better nature to assist me in my mission to save the life of my master. But the ruffian's reason had been driven out by drink, leaving only those dregs, those lesser demons that rule a man when his is in his cups.

'I have to go, I have an important message—' I began in an appealing tone. '—It is a matter of life and death. Truly, please let me pass.' I made to step out from under his arm but he caught hold of the blanket, wound it around his forearm, and pulled it tight. It came away and for an instant I broke free, but he anticipated the moved and grabbed my arms, banging me back against the door. The blow winded me and I struggled to catch my breath. My drunken companion laughed at my discomfort. 'Not so fast, my little pretty,' he slavered like a breathless dog. 'Did no one ever tell you it's rude to leave without first being introduced? Would you care to join my friend and me by the fire for a cup or two of the finest wine?'

Behind him the brazier spat and flared for an instant, and in the glow I knew I must seem the very thing the men had summoned from their basest fantasies.

My white petticoat was fashioned from the sheerest of fabrics, revealing every curve and plain of my body. Here and there it clung to my flesh where the fever from the potion had lifted dewy patches. The slob wiped the back of his hand across his mouth, his eyes flashing with drink driven lust.

'Please let me go,' I beseeched again, but knowing my words had fallen on deaf ears. 'I have to go. It really is a matter of the gravest urgency – of life and death.'

'Life and death, eh?' he said, rolling closer so I could feel his grotesque manhood pressing into my belly, and had to turn my face from his putrid breath. 'An angel, are you? Seems you've answered a journeyman's prayer tonight. Open your legs for me and show us a little piece of paradise, sweet angel.'

As he spoke his lips sought mine and his tongue drove

between them, while his hands mauled my breasts and he pressed his knee between my thighs. I tried to push him off, though I dare not scream out for fear of alerting the guards. If they took me back into the castle, fate might see to it that it was my ladyship and not my master who was informed of my plight – and then all hope would be lost. Even so, it was my instinct to fight.

I twisted away from my would-be seducer. To my horror he laughed and held me all the tighter by the shoulders. Looking back to his drunken compatriots, several of who were already on their feet, he beckoned them closer.

'Come here, Saob, and help me with this slippery little wench. And you, Francis and Leo. You shall all have your turn, or perhaps she has a few friends upstairs who would like the company of good men such as ourselves? What say you wench?'

'Please,' I begged, wriggling from his grasp, 'I am alone, please just let me go. I really have to go.' But my appeal was lost on him.

Saob, if indeed that was his name, was a rough giant of a man. He grabbed my arms and snatched them back behind me, while the first slob caught the fastenings at the neck of the petticoat and ripped it open to the waist.

His eyes widened at the sight of my naked breasts. The treacherous night air hardened the nipples instantly.

'Oh by Christ, such pretty, pretty jewels we have here,' he slobbered drunkenly, running his rough work-hardened palms over first one poor breast and then the other. He lifted one to his lips and drew the nipple deep into his mouth. 'Seems we have struck real lucky tonight, my old friend,' he mumbled thickly around the tormented bud.

Behind me, Saob slipped a hand across my ribs to join the slob in his explorations and cupped the other breast, while the first still sucked long and hard. This second man was older, thicker set, with a full beard and smelt of beer and sweat and tobacco. His younger companion, suckling still, made puppyish noises of pleasure as he ran his tongue around the hardened peak of my dugs.

'If you ask my opinion, young Jacob,' the older Saob slurred, 'there's plenty of her for us all. Get her on her hands and knees. Five of us can tup her at once if you know what you're doing. Get her down and I'll show you want I mean. Come on, she'll need to be well wet though.' He spat into the palm of his grubby hand.

Jacob pulled away and snorted, his top lip curling. 'You want to share her? All at once? I'd rather take turns, and as I found her I'll go first.' He turned his bleary attention to me, but still spoke to his companion, 'Just see this...' he croaked. While he'd been licking and tonguing my nipples he had gently slid his hand against my quim, where the moisture, I knew, already coated his thickset fingers. He lifted his hand to show those glistening fingers in the light of the fire and to prove he needed no assistance.

But to my horror, despite his refusal to share, his companion Saob pushed me down onto the rough soiled straw without any further ado. 'Just as you like, cousin, but let's get on with it. Night moves on and we've to be up early. You can have the wench first. Do as you will with her, and then the rest of us will take our turn. Nothing fires a man's blood like watching another tup a wet and willing wench. Away with you, boy, to the job in hand.'

Jacob dropped to his knees beside me and then sucked

on his fingers, slick with my juices, his face the image of pleasure. 'A fair deal, cousin. I would drink awhile at this particular well, I think.' He wriggled forward until he was between my legs, and spread me wide open.

If the truth were told I would wish to heaven that the events of the next few hours could be wiped from my mind, but it cannot be so. As the moon and the stars moved slowly through the firmament, I knew that whatever else happened I had to keep my wits about me so that when I had the chance, I could slip away from my lust driven captor. I prayed as Jacob pulled me closer that that moment would come soon.

Jacob eagerly lifted the tattered remains of my petticoat and slapped a wet kiss on the seat of his desire, breathing me in, his tongue working back and forth across that throbbing slit. His caresses went on and on until I thought I might die. If I had expected anything from my chance encounter with the drunken workmen, pleasure was most certainly not amongst the things it might have been.

While Jacob lapped at my quim, taking his fill, kneeling beside me, Saob caught hold of my hair and dragged my head into his lap, guiding his grizzled cock deep into my mouth with one meaty paw. I had little choice but to suck the old journeyman dry.

Jacob, meanwhile, had lit a beacon fire in my belly with his lips and tongue that threatened to rage out of control and engulf me. As I began to lose myself he thrust his fingers deep. My body grasped him tight, and then all was lost. Before the waves of pleasure had finished washing over me, Jacob spread my legs wide and mounted me, driving his raging shaft home, and then lifting my legs up onto his shoulders so he could drive deeper still. The man's thrusts were so fierce I bayed in pain, but this only seemed to egg him on.

In my mouth and under the touch of my fingertips, Saob began to thrust raggedly too, dragging me hard up against him, so when finally his seed pumped into my mouth he succeeded in almost choking me. But this was no more than a beginning.

Between my legs, Jacob took no more than seconds to follow Saob's example, and came with a vengeance, filling me to the brim with his frothing juices. I opened my eyes as the first intense waves of passion passed, and was stunned to find I was looking up into the faces of Jacob and Saob's compatriots and fellow travellers.

The unnerving huddle of men had the look of hounds on the scent of a young vixen; bright eyed, trembling with excitement, slavering over my exposed and sweating body.

And then, under Saob's watchful eye, they did indeed take their turns with me. One, two, three and more at a time, filling quim and mouth, hands and arse with their distended cocks, their filthy slack lips and kisses, their fingers molesting my breasts and belly. They were all over me, their raw animal passion so all-consuming I thought I was finally lost beneath a dark sea of unending, faceless, nameless desires.

By the time they were finally sated, there was no part of me, or my petticoat, no fold, no crease, no part of my body or soul that was not wet or stained with the seed of those wild, dark travelling men.

My saving grace was drink, for between each round with me they re-filled their flagons and drank deep and hearty. They had been drinking long before my untimely arrival and it is well know that strong drink and passion soon drives a man into a deep slumber. I struggled to keep my wits about me until Jacob finally pulled me close and threw his cloak over us both.

'Let us take a little sleep, lass,' he murmured, the words thick with beer and good wine. 'Soon we will begin again.'

As soon as his eyes, their lids so heavy, settled on his cheek I eased myself out from under his weighty arm, found the blanket he'd dragged off me earlier and, wrapping it tight around my shoulders, headed back to the castle.

It might be better to go back though the secret door. I was just pondering what best to do when, to my complete surprise, I saw a familiar figure sloping across the courtyard.

'Father Orme,' I whispered under my breath, a little afraid in case I woke the travellers. Clutching the blanket tight around me I hurried across the yard, managing to sidestep the sleepy guard who was accompanying the elderly priest without any difficulty.

'Father Orme, is that you?' I cried out in relief, catching hold of his robe.

'Get off me,' the old man snapped angrily, shaking my hand free. 'Alms will be given after morning prayers... get back. I'm now off to my bed. Guard! You...' He swung round to see me off with his staff, raised it, and then recognised my voice or me and stopped mid-swipe. 'My God! Beatrice, is that you?' he spluttered, waving the guard away. 'By all the saints, what has happened to you? Let me look at you, girl.'

He lifted the lantern he was carrying and peered at me. His face told me everything I need to know about my appearance. It was all too much. I staggered forward, feeling faint.

'I have to talk to my master,' I whispered, tears bubbling up behind my eyes. 'I have learnt this night of a plan to murder him. Please, Father, please take me to him. Her ladyship plans to have him killed at first light when he and Lord Usher go hunting. She has hired mercenaries to lay in wait by the river. I know it sounds like madness, but Arturo has betrayed him. Please Father, please.' The words tumbled out like water.

Orme's face softened. My legs finally buckled and he beckoned the guard closer to pick me up.

'Come back with me, child, and I will get you cleaned up. You are feverish.'

'You will tell him, won't you?' I begged, even as the darkness of unconsciousness threatened to engulf me.

'Yes, yes,' he asserted, but I feared he was just humouring me.

'If she succeeds,' I said as firmly as I could, 'she plans to have you killed too. She and Arturo have hired assassins from the house of Carun. She thinks it's your fault she had to wed in the first place, and wants you dead for it.'

At last I had the old man's undivided attention. Father Orme stared down at me. 'Does she indeed?' he said thoughtfully, rubbing his bony chin. 'Does she indeed?'...

Chapter Fifteen

Sarah pushed her chair away from the desk and stared at the computer screen, as if seeing it for the first time. She had typed every word of the doctor's carefully recorded translation in, but knew it had been an unthinking process; every shred of her consciousness, every molecule of thought and feeling had been with Beatrice de Fleur on her quest to save her master.

She felt tense and angry from reading of the poor girl's brave encounter with the drunken journeymen. And her stomach was knotted in case now, having escaped from her tormentors, Father Orme would not believe her, or help her by warning his lordship about the danger from Arturo and the hired assassins from the house of Carun.

What had dragged her away from the loose-leaf folder and the unfolding saga was the sound of the door opening. Sarah looked across the room, almost as if she was waking from a long, dream-filled sleep.

Chang indicated the landing. 'I thought we would go for a walk,' he said, waving her to her feet.

Sarah stared at him in total astonishment. 'A walk?' she repeated dumbly. It seemed such an unlikely thing for him to suggest, and the elegant red coat-dress and high heels she was wearing from the day before hardly seemed appropriate things to wear in the great outdoors.

But Chang could not be so easily dissuaded. 'That's right,' he said, holding out a hand in invitation. 'Oscar and me thought you might like the chance to explore the grounds while you're here.'

Sarah felt her colour draining, there was something about the way he spoke that suggested there was a lot more to his invitation than first appeared. She got to her feet unsteadily; sitting for so long without moving had given her pins and needles.

'I'll just get my jacket,' she said, indicating the wardrobe. 'I won't be a minute.'

Chang shook his head. 'You needn't bother,' he said mysteriously. 'You won't be requiring it.'

Sarah didn't know what to say to him, and decided on nothing.

He indicated the open door. 'If you please, the others are already waiting.'

When they got downstairs Sarah's worst suspicions were confirmed. Chang led her away from the main house along a broad, covered walkway that led down towards a vast greenhouse. Although sheltered from the autumn wind the walkway was far from warm.

The red dress seemed thin. Sarah shivered.

Chang waved her along. 'Not very much further now,' he said.

She glanced up. A little way ahead, Oscar, Oliver Turner's handsome Nordic chauffeur, was keeping watch by an ornate set of double doors that were designed to retain the heat and which led down into the hothouse.

He was dressed in cream jodhpurs and a crisp white open-necked shirt. He smiled warmly as she approached. 'You've still got a few minutes to get away,' he said with a grin, pushing the first of the doors ajar for her.

'I beg your pardon?'

Oscar pulled a face. 'To get away. Didn't Chang explain the rules to you? Amelia is already inside. Lots

184

of the others are in there too. You're the last of the hares to arrive.'

Still Sarah hesitated. She was totally confused.

'Hare and hounds, Miss Morgan,' Chang whispered menacingly. 'Perhaps you are familiar with the principles of the game? You run away and we give chase – it's simple enough. We always play in the glasshouse when we can. While the cats are busy in the big house, the mice – if you can call us that – take full advantage of whatever little diversions can be arranged.' He nodded at her high heels. 'I'd take those off if I were you. They'll make it very hard to run. Ah, here we are, the rest of the hounds have arrived.'

Sarah looked over her shoulder. Walking along the covered path towards them, with a strange and unnerving air of determination, were at least half a dozen other men of all shapes, sizes and ages. They were men she didn't recognise, but who she guessed were chauffeurs or valets; servants of Oliver Turner's guests.

Her jaw dropped and she instinctively backed away. Chang was deadly serious about the game. He and Oscar looked her up and down, and for the first time she saw they had the avaricious eyes of blood-lusting predators ready for the hunt.

She shot a fleeting glance at the approaching pack and sensed their blood was up. They were eager for the chase too, and she had no doubt they had all already imagined the pleasure and pain of what might follow when the hares were caught.

Some instinctive survival force switched on deep within her mind and before she quite knew what she was doing, she kicked off the shoes, pushed open the heavy door of the great glasshouse and hurried inside.

She ran down the first flight of steps onto a broad semi-circular brick paved area, set with palms in ornate tubs. The intense cloying blanket of humid heat hit her like a body blow. The air was heavy with the perfume of the flowers that clung to trelliswork suspended from the walls, and which grew up in stunning displays of pinks, yellows and oranges amongst the banks of foliage in enormous raised beds. The lush tropical heat was all-engulfing, and she was instantly bathed in a sheen of perspiration.

For a few seconds Sarah struggled to catch her breath and get her bearings, the blood pulsing in her ears as the first flood of adrenaline kicked in. There was an odd artificial quality to the light under the huge glass dome. The humidity in the hothouse was so high it muffled the sounds around her, and distorted them, so she couldn't fathom from which direction noises were coming. She was certain she could hear tumbling water, wild shrieks and cackling bird calls, or were they distant human voices? It was quite impossible to tell.

Leading away from the first brick terrace were winding gravelled paths to the left, right, and straight head of her, that led through a series of arches deeper into what looked for all the world like a tropical jungle. Each pathway was framed by great tumbles of glistening, dripping greenery, with fragrant creepers and convoluted vines heading skywards around them, curling up to the distant arc of the glazed roof.

Sarah glanced left and right, frantically trying to work out what to do. She couldn't risk staying too long on the terrace or any of the main paths. The hunt would surely soon begin, and they would find her in seconds if she stayed where she was. The narrow tailored skirt of the red coat-dress would make running impossible, its colour alone would give her away if she wanted to hide.

Guessing her pursuers would make short work of the dress when they caught her anyway, she hastily pulled it off and, rolling it into a bundle, dropped it in amongst a great clump of ferns, before heading off down the path to her left. As soon as she was through the first arch she scrambled up onto the raised planting area, pushed aside the plate-sized leaves of one of the bushes, and headed across the soft mulched forest floor, forcing herself further into the thick undergrowth.

In the wet heat the leather basque and sheer black stockings clung to her like a second skin, and in a peculiar way seemed deeply appropriate; crouched amongst the bushes, her head snapping from side to side as she listened to the unfamiliar sounds closing around her, she felt like a creature turned wild, a sleek animal.

Her breasts were flushed and heaved as she tried to tame her breathing. As she crouched stealthily amongst the sculptural spines and stems of the tropical plants, she could smell herself. It was like the musk of an animal, the soft sweetness of her sweat mixed with the deeper fragrance of her sex.

For a second or two Sarah closed her eyes and took a few deep breaths, fighting to steady her nerves. As she did she let those senses and instincts that normally lay suppressed come to the fore. She suddenly felt strangely alert and in tune with the sounds and the smells of the captive rainforest around her.

Sarah was aware she was not alone. She moved her head slowly, and there, scuttling between two great pillars that were covered in creepers, she snatched a darting glimpse of someone running for cover. A naked shoulder, a shock of golden brown hair, a fleeting impression of a lithe body, though from the little she saw she wasn't certain whether her fleet-footed companion was male or female.

She didn't wait to find out.

Crouching low, she worked her way even deeper into the enveloping undergrowth, with every sense straining to pick up the sounds of any approaching hunters.

But the hunters weren't as concerned about stealth as she anticipated. Just as she tucked herself down under the shelter of a great thicket there was the frantic baying of a hunting horn, and then the wild cries of the human hounds as they set off in search of their quarry.

The hunt was on.

Within seconds there seemed to be people running backwards and forwards along every path and crashing through the undergrowth around her. She heard a triumphant whoop as one of the hunters flushed the first prey from cover, and then a delighted cheer as the victim was caught or surrendered.

Oscar had told her it was a game, but even so, waiting in the damp shadows to be discovered was a nerve-wracking experience. Sarah looked left and right, her senses ablaze as she felt the panic and excitement knotting her stomach. Should she stay where she was and hope the hounds would pass her by, or dodge from bush to bush to try to evade them?

Making her snap decision and keeping low, Sarah bolted as quietly as she could towards the next thicket, and as she did she glanced down onto the main walkway. What she saw there made her stop in her tracks.

Chang had already caught his prey.

She was an exquisite androgynous creature, with long

tendrils of night-black hair that tumbled onto narrow shoulders. His catch was slim and sinuous and pale as moonlight, and truly did look at one with the dark shadows below the rainforest canopy.

Chang's face was set in a grimace as he struggled to hold his catch down. The figure was wriggling and squirming in his arms like a fish on a line. Naked except for a scrap of emerald-coloured cloth tied around her waist, his catch turned again, and Sarah saw it was a female, with strange haunted eyes of milky green. Given Chang's tastes and Sarah's memories of the anal dildo, she was a little surprised.

On the gravelled path the girl crouched like a cornered cat, growled at Chang, and tried to scratch his face. He grinned, and moved with surprising agility to avoid her claws. Grabbing her wrist, he twisted her round and pressed her down onto the path, lifting her arm up her back, and swiftly ripping away the shred of green cloth.

She cursed and squirmed and kicked out at him, but Chang had no problem in dodging the vicious swipes. His captive was built like a teenage boy; lean and lightly muscled, with small breasts. Her sex was shaved and one of the outer labia was pierced and adorned with a gold ring.

Chang jerked her up onto hands and knees, his palm's cupping those tiny tits, nipping and working at the hardened peaks. His prey struggled valiantly against him, although even as they fought, Sarah could sense the girl's growing arousal as the erotic game unfolded.

'Be still,' Chang ordered breathlessly. 'I've caught you, you know that... stop fighting.'

The girl swore and strained again in a final feeble attempt to break free, but Sarah sensed it was more of a gesture than true resistance.

The girl was wet between her legs, her sex glistening with excitement. Chang pushed her face down towards the pea gravel. 'Submit, you little bitch,' he grunted. 'You know what I want, Lola, and you know you want it too.'

The girl shot him a glance over her shoulder, and then, to Sarah's shock, she giggled, her green eyes alive with mischief.

'Okay... I submit,' she purred, and ran a finger through the wet lips of her quim. 'So what would you like?'

Chang grunted again, his eyes sparkling and bright with need. To Sarah, peering through the lush leaves from her hiding place, it was clear the thrill of the chase – however short – had warmed Chang's blood. He leant into the bushes and pulled out a long supple cane, and as he did he glanced up momentarily and caught sight of Sarah spying on them. He grinned and then turned his attention back to the panting Lola.

Coming face to face with her tormentor Sarah felt her composure slipping away. She froze, searching for what to do. Should she run, and risk being caught by the other hunters? Or should she remain in the undergrowth and hope Chang would satisfy himself with the feline Lola?

Her mind was a blur, and she remained rooted to the spot.

Lola settled herself on all fours, her face raised and her eyes closed, waiting quietly for Chang's next move. The cane lifted, Sarah held her breath, and then watched, mesmerised, as it swished down and exploded across the girl's milky flesh—

The shriek was instantly smothered into a muffled whimper as a hand clamped painfully over Sarah's mouth and an arm locked around her ribs and squeezed the breath out of her lungs. Her nostrils flared as she inhaled desperately.

'Like to watch, do you?' a fearsome voice hissed in her ear. She tried to struggle, but it was hopeless; whoever was holding her was far too strong. She could feel the heat of his breath rasping against her cheek, the steady beat of his heart against her back, and the brazen press of his erection against her hip. The thrill of the chase had certainly heated his blood.

'Turn her round, Bradbury,' snapped another voice from close by. 'Let the dog see the rabbit. Come on.'

Sarah's heart raced; there were two of them. She wondered if Chang had seen them creeping up on her and it had been this, and not recognition, that had made him grin.

She willed herself to relax, and felt the tension in her captor's arms do likewise. Suddenly sensing a fleeting opportunity, she twisted and lunged forward. The hold broke and, amazed she had succeeded in breaking free, she darted away into the dense cover of the bushes.

'Why, you little bitch,' he roared after her, though she sensed it was as much with delight as anger.

'What happened?' shouted the second man.

'Nothing. Let's get after her.'

Sarah dodged and ducked, turned this way and that, but she knew they were still close behind. She threw a feint to the left and then turned right, scrambling between the trees and climbers, afraid to look back, running low and fast. As she broke out into the open and crossed one of the paths she turned for the briefest of instants to see if they were gaining, and in that split second she lost her footing, staggered, and fell forward. With hands outstretched she tried to break her fall, but she crashed into green foliage which parted under the assault and she plunged helplessly into a pool of cascading water. The cold shock made her gasp, and she bobbed to the surface spluttering and coughing, trying to clear her lungs.

She had stumbled clumsily into an enormous pond, backed by an ornamental waterfall. Her feet couldn't touch the bottom, so she started swimming for the far side. A whoop and a splash behind her and she knew one of her pursuers had followed her in. She lengthened her stroke, but fatigue was taking its toll. The sounds of rhythmic splashing grew louder in her ears and she knew he was closing. As she tried to swim faster her stroke became more and more ragged and water shipped into her gaping mouth as she tried to fill her burning lungs. At last her toes touched the bottom and she managed to wade towards the side, her arms flailing in her exhaustion. She glanced back over her shoulder. The man was ploughing through her wake towards her. He was powerfully built, muscular, and covered in thick dark hair that formed a mat over his shoulders and stout arms. For some reason Sarah couldn't move. She stood like a frightened rabbit and watched as the man emerged and stood in front of her, the water lapping around their middles. His torso dripped and gleamed, the hair now slick like a thick pelt.

Sarah did nothing to protect herself as he reached out, gripped the back of her neck, and pulled her close. He kissed her hungrily, staking his claim. She shivered and found herself responding, completely overwhelmed by his presence and strength.

'Okay, okay, Bradbury,' called someone from the edge of the pool. 'Leave a little of that for me.' It was the voice Sarah had heard in the bushes. The accent was American, whiny and thin. Her captor broke off the kiss and Sarah looked in the direction of the voice. There was a small man gazing appreciatively down at her. He was not good-looking, and in the latter years of his life. Wisps of grey hair struggled to cover his balding pate and a scrawny beard sprouted from a large chin. Sarah gasped, for he was flexing a cane between gnarled fists.

'Come on, Bradbury,' he urged, 'get her out of there. She looks a tasty little morsel and I want some fun.'

The younger captor turned her and pushed her towards the side where his companion stood. Her arms were squeezed behind her back, thrusting her breasts towards the greedy eyes of the waiting man, and Sarah realised just how excited she now was to be at the mercy of these two. She couldn't tear her gaze from the whippy length of wood

As they reached the side she could do nothing as her strong captor lifted her up onto one of the large flat rocks that edged the pool. Sarah looked down at her dripping body. Her stockings were ruined, torn to shreds by the chase through the undergrowth, and the leather basque was smeared with grime.

'You belong to Casswell, right?' he panted, still a little out of breath after the exhilaration of the chase.

There was little use her denying it. She nodded.

He grinned and nodded his approval. 'That's what we thought. The fellow certainly has good taste when it comes to women.' He levered himself out of the water and onto the rock beside her. He was naked! Sarah turned her head and tried not to look, but the dark hair on his chest extended down over his belly, and drew her eyes lower still to a large penis that nestled sleepily in his groin. The sheer size of it made her tremble. She blushed and quickly averted her gaze.

She looked up at him, trying hard to disguise the eagerness and hunger in her eyes. Bradbury grinned and shook his head.

'You have to earn it, baby,' he teased, making her cringe at being so transparent. 'And believe me, you will.'

He twisted her and pushed her forward, face down. He nudged her legs apart and stripped off the remains of her stockings. Deftly, he tied her hands with one, and then blindfolded her with the other. His standing companion watched patiently, thoughtfully flexing the cane, as she was prepared.

Bradbury backed away and left her alone for a few seconds. Time was suspended as she waited, and then she heard the swish – for an instant it seemed unrelated to anything – and the cane exploded across her buttocks and drilled into her brain like nothing she had ever known in her life. The man certainly knew how to wield the tortuous implement. The cruel and unjust pain was excruciating. Her back arched and her shoulders lifted as she wailed for mercy.

Unbeknown to the sobbing girl, Chang was watching from the cover of some nearby rare and exotic shrubs. Finished with beating and screwing the very accommodating arse of the beautiful and imaginative Lola, he observed Sarah's writhing submission with a great deal of interest and enjoyment. Every detail of the girl's caning was committed to memory, and would regurgitated blow by blow, shriek by shriek, for his master's pleasure later in the day.

Doctor Casswell, he knew, would be delighted by his

student's progress, but also a little disappointed not to have witnessed the events for himself, either in person or on close-circuit TV.

From his vantage point, hidden amongst the undergrowth, Chang could see Sarah on the rock, tied and blindfolded. She shrieked again and again as the cane skilfully found its mark. Every sinew in her body tautened as the pain ricocheted through her prone body.

Chang smiled. The beating went on until the valet, Butt, judged she had taken enough and his arm ached.

There was a pregnant pause while the two men silently savoured her submissive beauty, their eyes consistently drawn to the irregular pattern of red welts that enhanced the loveliness of her creamy buttocks, and then Bradbury carefully rolled her onto her back. She winced as the cold stone came into contact with her beaten flesh, but she made no protest as he pushed her trembling thighs apart and began to nuzzle and lick at the juicy contours of her welcoming sex. The smears of grime emphasised her pallor. She was already excited, and moaned with a mixture of surprise, relief, and hunger as his tongue wormed into her. She would have to be well lubricated to take the monster that sprouted from between the bodyguard's muscular thighs.

The hairy man tested her with strong fingers, first one and then two, whispering to her, encouraging her, until finally she was ready and he sank his rigid shaft to the hilt in her wet and clutching vagina.

Sarah began to move against him, tentatively at first, but with growing confidence as her body relaxed and opened up to ease his progress.

Chang could see she was on the brink of a mighty orgasm, while with every plunge of his muscular buttocks, Bradbury ploughed deeply and rapidly approached his own climax.

The watching Oriental smiled; Sarah Morgan had done exactly what was asked of her without a second's hesitation. She was learning fast.

Chapter Sixteen

In the main house the conference had already broken for lunch. Rigel Casswell picked up a plate from the buffet table and, after filling it from the opulent spread of food on offer, made his way towards Oliver Turner, who was holding court with Lassiter and Ford. Around the elegant dining room little groups had formed into huddles. He heard snatches of their conversations as he passed; everyone was talking about the diary and expounding their own personal views on its authenticity.

During the second session of the morning's conference news about the book had been very mixed indeed, and there was a distinct air of dejection amongst some of the delegates.

Yes, Beatrice de Fleur's diaries had most certainly existed at the turn of the century, that point was not really under debate. But there was very little evidence to support the view that the book in the possession of Turner and Casswell was part of that well-documented collection.

Even the construction of the book itself added another layer of ambiguity to their quest for the truth. One of the speakers, a German professor called Gilim, had argued the book was made of genuine materials from the period. But then, playing devil's advocate, he explained it was possible, if one knew the right supplier, to buy unused parchment, vellum, in fact whatever was required from the appropriate period to make a masterful fake.

Relatively cheaply too. And, in his view, there were certain factors about Beatrice's diary that indicated that such a scenario seemed possible – even likely.

There had been gasps of surprise and dismay from the assembled audience. Above him, slides of pages from the manuscript had clicked into place and he began to point out some of the anomalies that concerned him most.

There were several clues Gilim said: in the fabric of the making, something about the manner of stitching and the thread used, and in the document, in the body of the text itself, the way in which certain letters had been formed and certain words used. It appeared to Gilim that the scribe had no real concept or understanding of what he was writing, but was just copying blind, so to speak. If it had been a failing on the part of the original writer, through poor education or some personal foible, then the mistakes would be habitual and occur again and again in the same context – and they did not.

Oliver Turner was trying to put a brave face on it, though he couldn't quite hide his disappointment. He lifted his arms, miming resignation; there would be other diaries, even other parts to this one, many other erotic treasures for him to hunt down, he said with a confident smile. He'd go off in search of those if the diary Rigel Casswell was busy translating turned out to be a clever fake…

Casswell cringed as his mind formed the word 'fake'. He tried to force his attention onto his lunch and stabbed at a wafer-thin curl of the finest smoked salmon. It tasted fine enough, but couldn't quite still his busy thoughts.

Just thinking about the possibility of the book being a fake made him uneasy. Although he'd known from the beginning it was a very real possibility. As he'd worked on the text he'd become entranced by the compelling magic of Beatrice de Fleur's voice.

The diary had seemed almost too complete, too fresh to be a fake. But then, Casswell thought with a wry smile, those were the very qualities any good forger would employ to make it so convincing.

He took a sip of his wine and glanced out across the rolling lawns towards Oliver's glasshouse tucked away behind an impressive windbreak of poplars. From this distance the tropical house looked like an enormous circus tent constructed from glass. Mid-morning sunshine reflected off its great roof. Perhaps, he thought, the smile on his face broadening, he would have been better employed out there this morning with Chang, Sarah and others. In his mind's eye, Beatrice de Fleur and the discovery and education of Sarah Morgan were somehow inexplicably linked.

Oliver Turner beckoned him closer. The delegates were all waiting for Sir Egon Howard to arrive from Florence. He had already rung from the airport to say he would be arriving at the mansion after lunch. Perhaps he could bring something a little more definite and uplifting to the table.

Casswell drained his glass. 'So, how goes it, Oliver?'

The elderly gentleman, who at his approach had carefully extricated himself from the circle of guests, smiled grimly. 'Good manners preclude my answering honestly. I suppose I should have prepared myself for this, but it hurts. What say you and I go and get a snifter of brandy?'

Casswell nodded and followed his host out towards the study.

In the tropical house Sarah rolled over onto her back, gasping, feeling the last remnants of orgasm pulsing through her sex like a rogue heartbeat. She wondered how much longer the two men, so dissimilar in build yet so alike in appetite, could go on. Bradbury, the younger and the larger of the two, had made love to her twice now with that pendulous cock of his, performing under the watchful eyes of the older man, Butt.

The old man had also made love to her. They had untied her by the time he took his turn and the blindfold had worked lose, so Sarah lay back on the hard rock while the wizened man took her. He had grunted and struggled his way to orgasm, while Bradbury looked on, holding tight to Sarah's wrists in case she tried to escape, while at the same time lazily stroking her breasts and caressing her face. In spite of everything it had proved to be a heady combination.

Butt was a skilled lover. What he lacked in stamina he more than made up for with experience and technique. His hips ground into hers, his pubic ridge pressed down into her sex, making her wail and writhe with excitement.

As he had coaxed her towards a wonderful orgasm, she had been aware, through misty eyes, of another hare being brought down by a handsome and feverish hound nearby. It could have been Amelia who was caught, but it was hard to tell.

After a short spell to recover, Bradbury lumbered to his feet and spoke to his companion. 'One more dip in the bran tub, eh? See what we can pull out?'

Butt nodded, and without so much as a backward glance at the lovely exhausted girl, the two of them headed off down one of the paths back into the verdant undergrowth.

Sarah realised with a jolt that not only were they done with her, but that all around the glasshouse the game was still on, and that being caught once did not excuse her from being caught again. She looked anxiously left and right, praying no one could see her there on the rock.

She felt bedraggled. The soft leather basque was all but ruined now. Her stockings had long since been discarded. Her backside still throbbed from the application of the cane, and between her legs she felt a little tender.

Slipping stealthily from the rocks and into the soothing water she let its soft caress embrace and cool her punished body. She slowly swam out into the bubbling depths and then drifted towards the cover of some overhanging vines.

'Time to go back to the house,' called a familiar voice from the edge.

Sarah twisted in the water. Chang was standing there and holding out a white towelling robe. She couldn't help but smile; the little Oriental looked for all the world like some strange maiden aunt, come to collect her from her mid-morning dip. Without a second thought she swam towards him. However odd it seemed, Sarah knew she really was relieved to see him.

Once they were back in the main house, Chang ran a deep foamy bath and gently washed away the remnants of dirt and passion, his fingers working into her aching frame like some glorious, magical panacea. No more solicitous a body-servant could a girl want. When he was done he brought her up a tray of lunch, after which she went to bed. But before sleep called she caught sight of the diary lying on the desk by the computer, and knew she couldn't rest until she found out what had happened to Beatrice.

Wrapped in the duvet Sarah curled up to read the final few pages of Doctor Casswell's translation:

...When I finally awoke my first thoughts were of the dream I had been having. It was a terrible, terrible nightmare about death and rape, and men with swords, and murder. And then, as is sometimes the way upon waking, true life and reality filled me, and I knew with a sickening certainty that it had not been a dream at all. It was all I could do to stop myself from leaping up from the bed in fear and in panic. I struggled to make some sense of my bearings.

I was in Father Orme's quarters deep within the castle walls. Although it appeared stark and monastic, the unbleached linen on the priest's narrow bed was spun from the finest flax. And the bed itself, though simple in design, had been carved by a master. Poverty, it appeared, like chastity, was very much in the eye of the beholder.

At the sound of my movements, a young monk appeared from a curtained alcove across the dimly lit chamber. He was dressed in the distinctive habit of Orme's order, and although he looked no older than I, he had a serious and unmoving face that spoke of a life already dedicated to unwavering devotion and penitence. There was a certain arrogance about his bearing that was at odds with his calling. He looked down at me, unable to disguise his contempt and disgust.

'You are awake then.'

Unsteadily, I pulled myself up onto my elbows, aware that the boy's eyes lingered a little too long on the ripe swell of my breasts where they pressed up against the fine linen sheets.

'Has Father Orme gone to warn his lordship?' I asked

anxiously. 'Do you know if he has taken my message?'

The boy shrugged. 'I really have no idea, girl. The Abbe asked me to watch over you, to keep you safe and to see to such things as you might need,' he paused, reddening furiously. He clearly believed that such duties were far beneath him. 'He said I am to do as you command me. Strikes me as pure folly. 'Tis a bizarre commission for one of my calling, but then Father Orme trusts me to do as he commands,' he paused again, his voice tailing off, and I saw his gaze was still fixed on my body.

To one side of the narrow bed a tiny oil-lamp illuminated the chamber and the sheet, and for the first time I realised the young monk must be able to see my body picked out in silhouette through the fine cloth. He flushed scarlet when he guessed I had caught him out, and looked down at the worn flagstone floor.

'So what would you like?' he stammered, avoiding my gaze. 'Food? A little wine? Or perhaps I should rekindle the fire. There is a real nip in the air that chills even my bones.'

I glanced around. The remains of the ragged, stained petticoat and cloak were gone, but even so I could still smell the sweat and seed of Jacob, Saob and his compatriots clinging to my flesh. So I bade the lusty young monk bring me a large jug of hot water, a bowl, and some towels.

He seemed relieved to excuse himself from the room and returned a few minutes later with the things I had requested, together with a long nightshirt, the origins of which I can only guess. And then he withdrew again to let me bathe my weary body in peace.

But, left alone, my mind began to race. The old priest's

bedchamber was windowless, rendering me unable to fathom the hour. Would Orme get to my master in time? What if he was intercepted by his betrayer, Arturo, and that band of hired thugs? What would happen when her ladyship returned to her chamber and discovered I was missing – if she had not already?

After all, the night must have given way to the first light of dawn by now, and with it the departure of the ill-fated hunting party. It was almost more than my mind could bear. Anxiously, I called out to the young monk to ask what hour of the clock it was. But instead of answering from the anteroom, as I had anticipated, he swept aside the curtain and his eyes drank in the vision before him.

I was standing in the bowl of water, by a little table, washing myself with a rag, naked save for a thick linen towel I had snatched up to cover my nakedness as he stepped into the room.

My body glistened with the mixture of water and the sweet smelling unguents he had brought for me to use as part of my toilet.

For a few seconds the boy stood transfixed in the chamber doorway, taking in the details of my undress like a starving man at a banquet, and then his young face contorted with a strange mixture of lust and fury and his eyes reduced to pin-pricks of reflected light.

'You unholy vixen,' he snorted. 'Have you done this to undo me? You truly are a painted harlot. You think to bewitch all men with your unnatural beauty, oh Jezebel. May all the saints protect me from temptations of the flesh.' He looked heavenwards in desperation. But before I could answer or dissuade him he leapt forward, sweat beading his brow, and grabbed me by the shoulders, forcing me back onto the narrow bed, upsetting the bowl all over the flag floors.

I stumbled and slipped as he fell on top of me, breathing hard.

'I should beat the devil out of that evil flesh,' he hissed furiously.

'Get off me,' I gasped, struggling to unseat him. 'Please brother, I mean no harm either to your body or your soul. I was just washing. Get off me now and I'll say nothing to the good Father. You shouldn't have come in. I only wanted to know what time of day it was. Please... please... leave me be.'

But I might have saved what breath I could muster under his weight. He didn't hear a word of my appeal. Instead he stared down at me, glassy-eyed.

'Tell me truthfully if thou art a demon or some enchantress come to steal my virtue?' he hissed. 'Or are you temptation itself, setting a trap for the unwary soul – laid by that old devil Orme to test my calling? Tell me harlot, tell me!'

Before I could reply he began to wail, and his hands fell upon my breasts, squeezing and mauling as if he was possessed, while his mouth and teeth worked furiously over my damp flesh, biting and nipping at my body like some rabid dog.

What the young monk would not do was look me in the eye, as he forced my thighs apart and tried without success to press his already inflated pizzle into my quim. As I grabbed at him to try and push him off he looked away, as if he feared my gaze might enchant him. Or was it perhaps that he feared he might see his own lust reflected in my eyes?

His fingers breached me, dipping into that hot pit that

mesmerises men, and as he did he began to sob, 'Save me from this evil magic. Save me.' He plunged his fingers deeper still. His thumb brushed my pleasure bud more by accident than design and my body tightened around him. To my horror he threw back his head and howled like a wolf.

He caught hold of my hair and forced me down onto the wet flagstone floor, and snatching up a stick from the fireplace he began to beat me, the wood cracking and splintering across my buttocks. At last, when I could barely take another stroke, he fell to his knees and took me from behind like a dog, crouched there amongst the wreckage of the bowl, the jug, and the water. Even then he could not bring himself to touch his excited member and caught hold of my hand to help guide him in. As my fingers closed reluctantly around his shaft he sighed with pleasure and began to breathe hard and fast.

As my body opened for him, his cock thrust home and he began to pump furiously, as if he was being pursued by the very devil himself. As he finally found a rhythm he gripped my hips and pulled me onto him. Back to belly he was spared any possibility of our eyes meeting, and that I might see his need. And so, freed from his own guilt and anguish, the young monk drove on now, on and on and on, forcing his cock so deep he made me cry out.

Eventually I felt him shudder and then begin to pump in earnest. All guilt, all fear, all thoughts of the divine were lost as his body responded to the driving beat of a more ancient drum.

When the boy was done, his passion spent, he slipped out of me and hastily clambered to his feet.

'I will bring you some food and get this fire lit,' he

murmured as he straightened his habit, still not meeting my eyes.

Hastily I began to repair the damage his desire had wreaked on both my body and Orme's monastic chamber. I picked up the jug, cleaned up the tangle of wet towels, and pulled on the nightshirt to cover my nakedness.

I had barely completed my task when the curtain was pulled aside. I froze, wondering what fresh mischief my young monk might be at. But to my great relief it was Father Orme returning, although he seemed completely oblivious to the dishevelled state of his bedchamber.

He looked tired. His weather-beaten face was the colour of old marble.

'We have to go soon,' he said, indicating the door. He glanced for a moment at my scant clothing. 'I will have my boy find you a decent cloak and some sandals. I hope he has taken good care of you while I've been gone.'

I looked up. If only Orme knew. The young monk, who had reappeared through the curtain and now stood obediently at his master's shoulder, shot me a warning glance.

'Have you eaten?' the old man asked, looking at the little side-tables, still damp with soapy water.

I stared at Orme, hoping he might offer some shred of comfort or some word of what was going on in the rest of the castle, but he seemed immeasurably preoccupied.

'Father,' I began, trying hard to keep tight control of my mind, 'what news is there of my master?' I could hardly bear to form the thoughts, less still the words. 'My lord, is he…' my voice faded to a stifled sob as Orme focused on me for the first time and saw the expression of fear in my eyes.

To my great relief, he smiled, though it did little to

soften his grizzled countenance. 'Have no fear. He is well, child, though his heart is greatly saddened by the terrible events of this morning.'

Arturo had been his friend since childhood. The traitor is dead now, killed by one of the guards with a single sword blow. As were half the hired thugs. His lordship feels the Lady Elizabeth turned Arturo's loyalties; even a betrayer can be mourned. And the Lady Elizabeth is even now confined to her quarters under close guard. It seems that at last she will have her wish to go into a convent. Though we must be very careful what is said within the walls, after all, she is still mother to his lordship's children.'

Orme reached out and stroked a damp curl away from my cheek. 'He owes you his life, Beatrice, and I too.'

My eyes were damp with tears. 'May I go to him?'

Orme nodded slowly. 'Aye, I think it would please him to see you. Usher is keeping company with him now. Come, let us find you a good cloak and we will be away.'

He beckoned to the boy monk who even now refused to meet my eye.

'Get the Lady Beatrice a warm mantle and then see to it that we have some food sent up to his lordship's apartment. It has been a long night and I am famished.'

I followed Orme through the castle. It was barely light, and around us the rest of those who had spent the night safe under the walls were just stirring into life, oblivious as yet to the drama that had been acted out under the shadow of their slumbers.

My stomach tightened with every step, and with my heart beating like a drum in my chest we finally reached my lordship's chambers.

Orme bade the guard let us through, and then called

out to let his lordship know we were coming. Inside the main room my master sat in a great chair by the hearth, wrapped in a fur cloak against the cold of the new dawn and flanked by his cousin, Lord Usher. He looked up briefly at the sound of our footfalls, and for an instant I saw him as if for the first time. He seemed to have aged in those few short hours, the handsome lines and firm jaw suddenly haggard and grey, while the light in his eyes seemed faded and sad. And then he focused on my face and my heart leapt. He smiled and the years fell away.

He stood up and opened his arms, and I without a second's hesitation ran to him, longing to feel his embrace, his power, and the warmth of his body next to mine.

'You will come whenever I call for you, Beatrice,' he said in a broken emotional tone, echoing the words he had spoken to me on that first day in his chamber. How far we had come since then. 'I will brook no excuses, girl, no delays. You are mine now, do you understand?'

I nodded, unable to find the words to reply, and clung to him instead. His features had softened. His eyes, so steely before, were gentle now.

'Remember who you serve, lady. I am your only master. Our fates are closely entwined, Beatrice. Yours and mine.'

And for the first time I understood exactly what he meant. I had come home.

Chapter 16

Sarah closed the book and wiped away a tear. She was sad that the account had finally ended, and yet at the same time deeply relieved that Beatrice de Fleur had been reunited with her master, and that both of them were safe and well.

The guest bedroom in Oliver Turner's mansion was dark now, the last light of the afternoon finally fading to a rich autumnal gold. She wondered for the first time in many hours how Doctor Casswell was fairing downstairs in the conference room with Oliver Turner's team of experts. It seemed an age since she had seen or spoken to him, but even so, the mere thought of his cruelly handsome face lit a tiny beacon in her belly. Like Beatrice de Fleur, Sarah considered him to be her master, her lord, and the realisation made her shiver.

She slipped off the bed and looked at herself in the dressing table mirror. The fading light of the day picked out the glimmer of desire in her eyes. She ran her hands over her hips and thighs, turning to admire the uplift of her exquisite breasts and the soft swell of her belly.

Her body was still marked by the raw tracks of Butt's cane, and the outline of the brand still glowed raw and uncomfortable on her flank. Here and there were scratches and bruises from her chase through the tropical house. Yet for all this she knew she had a sensual beauty that both surprised and delighted her. It would be hard to disguise outside the confines of the hedonistic life Doctor Casswell had introduced her to.

She leant over and tugged the bell-pull a couple of times, summoning Chang from wherever he had spent his afternoon. Perhaps, she thought with a wry smile, he might be cracking another bottle of brandy with Oscar, Oliver Turner's handsome Nordic chauffeur, exchanging stories about what had gone on in the tropical house.

Chang appeared a few minutes later carrying a tea

tray.

'I take it you slept well?' he said, setting it down on a side-table and nodding at the tumble of sheets and duvet on the large bed.

Sarah was sitting in a chair by the window, looking out into the rapidly darkening evening. Across the vast expanse of lawns and gardens a network of paths were picked out by strings of silver lights that looked uncannily like a pearl necklace in the increasing gloom. One path that caught her eye led down to the tropical house.

'I didn't sleep at all,' she said, after a second or two. 'I read the rest of the diary. I had to see how it ended. I'll type up the transcript first thing tomorrow.'

Chang shook his head. 'There may not be any need. The German professor, Gilim, thinks the whole thing is probably a fake.'

Sarah was shocked. She struggled to catch her breath. 'Are you serious?' she asked, her feelings of disappointment immense. Since she had first arrived at Casswell Hall, Beatrice de Fleur's compelling story had formed a framework to her own initiation and training at Doctor Casswell's masterly hands. The girl's amazingly erotic tale and Sarah's life had become interwoven and were, at least in her mind, totally inseparable.

Chang nodded and poured the tea. 'Yes. They're all still waiting downstairs for some expert to arrive from Florence. He phoned to tell them he had some very important information. He should have been here after lunch, but his plane was delayed.' The little Oriental paused and looked her up and down. 'I think it's about time you prepared yourself for Mr Turner's little supper party.'

211

Sarah was wrapped in a white silk robe that she'd found hanging on the bathroom door. Chang beckoned her to her feet, and she did as she was bidden without a second's hesitation and turned slowly under his dark unfathomable eye.

He nodded his approval. Exquisitely made, the scant garment was so short it barely covered her bottom and was so sheer that every curve and plain of her body showed through – almost as if she had been gift-wrapped in white silk.

'Is Doctor Casswell all right?' she asked as she turned around, hoping Chang would not punish her for speaking out of turn, and yet also aware of the tiny but intense pulse of desire that her master's name evoked. Sarah knew she had changed immeasurably in the past few days; it hadn't occurred to her to get dressed or cover herself before the Oriental arrived.

For once Chang ignored her breaking the rules. 'I would imagine so. Would you like to shower while I lay out your clothes for this evening?'

Sarah stared at him in surprise. He spoke without emotion, and for the first time it was quite obvious to Sarah that he really had no idea of the power the diary wielded over both her and Doctor Casswell.

Part of her wished for nothing more than to go to find the doctor, just like Beatrice had gone with Father Orme to comfort her master. She looked at Chang, wondering if he could read her thoughts and if not, if she could muster the courage to ask him to take her to the doctor. Chang looked away and she knew the moment was lost.

Minutes later Sarah was in the shower. The water coursed down over her body, the warmth easing into the aching muscles almost as effectively as Chang's knowing fingers. But for all the relief the water gave her, it was difficult to think about anything other than his words regarding Beatrice's diary.

As she stepped from the shower and wrapped herself in a towel, Chang stood in the bathroom doorway, watching her. In one hand he was holding a mask, set with diamanté, and curling black feathers.

'Part of your costume for tonight,' he said without emotion. 'Quickly now, they'll be waiting for you.'

Downstairs in the garden room, Oliver Turner refilled Rigel Casswell's champagne flute. Both men glanced around the shadowy interior. Turner had wanted to make sure everything was ready for the arrival of his guests. He had already settled on a medieval theme, to echo the history of the diaries, before they had heard the delegates' findings. Perhaps it might have been wiser to have chosen something else – but it was too late now.

The elongated room was divided by a row of ornate columns that supported the glass roof, and from these had been hung great garlands of ivy and lanterns. Set with a row of trestle-tables and benches the whole room resembled a medieval banqueting hall. Rigel Casswell sipped his champagne. Already a couple of the other delegates were busy at the bar. He wondered if they had decided to drown their sorrows. All afternoon the atmosphere had been more than a little subdued, and Egon Howard had still not arrived from Florence with his very important news – damn the man.

Turner lifted a hand in greeting to two of his guests. Crouched beside the two delegates were their body slaves, both naked chained and masked. One – a thin boy with a shock of blond hair – sported a flurry of strange ritual tattoos over his arms and legs that gave him an almost serpentine quality. The second was a girl of mixed race whose skin had been oiled so it looked as though she was carved from an exotic golden wood.

As Casswell looked at her she glanced up at him and smiled, revealing a row of pearly-white teeth. Her eyes were dark and leonine, as black and untamed as a forest night. As she stretched and eased the heavy chain that joined her to her master, Casswell could see that her body was scarified; her face, arms and breasts were covered in complex swirling spirals of scars that were at once both fascinating and deeply disturbing.

The band began to play, and Casswell and Turner turned their attention to the buffet that lined one wall.

'Lonely?' whispered a familiar voice from behind them. Both men turned to look into the masked eyes of a slim blonde creature dressed in an exquisite peacock-blue silk corset. It was laced tightly, emphasising her slim waist and full hips and breasts. Delicate wisps of lace barely covered her nipples, and she wore black silk stockings that were held up with lace garters, and high heeled lace-up ankle boots. Intricate ringlets twisted into a tumble of blonde hair framed a matching peacock mask.

Oliver Turner smiled, and leaning forward, pressed a kiss to Amelia's cheek, while at the same time he slid his fingers up over her thighs. Amelia smiled and then wriggled closer, her long slim legs opening a little to give the elderly gentleman easier access.

'I missed you too,' she purred, licking her lips like some sleek, well-fed feline. She began to rub herself against him, her sinuous body moving sexily in time to the music.

Amused by her delicious performance, Casswell shook

his head and looked away, leaving the two of them to their well-rehearsed erotic game. He glanced at his watch. Chang should be upstairs preparing Sarah Morgan for the party. All he had to do was wait and watch the comings and goings of his fellow guests. And there was much to observe.

Around him the garden room was rapidly filling up. Although the air amongst the guests was still subdued, the arrival of the delegates' slaves was gradually, subtly altering the atmosphere. Each slave represented some part of their master's fantasies, and they certainly reflected a stunning array of tastes. They were exotic, outrageous, bizarre, and utterly, utterly compelling.

The music drew a handful of dancers out onto the floor. Some were naked and some were dressed, and there was every shade in between.

At the bar stood Doctor Ford, who had brought twins back from his last trip to the Far East. The two delicate Oriental sisters, naked except for their masks, collars, and silver patent high heeled pumps, waited like puppy's at the end of their leash for their master to command them. Across the room, Leonra Stevenson, one of the few female delegates, was dancing to the strains of the band, accompanied by her boy, who was dressed as a medieval minstrel, complete with bulging codpiece.

Casswell glanced at his watch again, and when he looked up, saw Sarah Morgan framed in the open doorway. Led by Chang, who was dressed in a simple black silk Mao jacket, the girl looked stunning. On the end of a fine silver chain that was attached to her collar, she was wearing a close-fitting bodysuit that was covered in sleek black feathers. Combined with the mask, it made her look like some wonderful exotic bird.

The bodice had long sleeves, and the fabric thinned over her exquisite breasts so that her nipples peaked through the finer, silken fabric. She wore black stockings, and the pale swell of her sex was framed in a tumble of black silk and curling feathers that reflected inky shades of green and blue in amongst the coal-black fronds. The whole outfit offered a heady invitation to linger and explore further.

Rigel Casswell smiled.

From behind her mask Sarah stared around the room. It was as though she had been washed up on the darkest shores of passion.

Doctor Casswell extended a hand and took the fine silver lead from Chang. 'Good evening, my dear. You look very beautiful.'

Sarah nodded, feeling unable to speak. Her silent acknowledgement of his compliment appeared to please him. Oliver Turner looked at her also. She could sense his delight with what he saw as too.

Sarah glanced uncertainly around the party again. The other slaves were all stunning and exuded an intimidating sexuality, dressed in fantasy costumes, all beautifully made-up and coiffeured. They were as exotic and enticing as the sumptuous buffet arranged behind Casswell and Turner.

Other delegates had looked up upon her arrival. They must have known she was new, and although their glances were covert, it didn't quite disguise the fact that many appraised her body with the eyes of potential purchasers.

Outside, beyond the huge glass windows, the night sky was a cloudless band of stars, while inside a *frisson* of electric desire was slowly bubbling to the surface. It was not overtly seductive as yet, but possessed an intense erotic promise of things to come. Sarah shivered, trying hard to control the wild fluttering in her stomach.

Amelia uncurled herself from Turner and ran a teasing finger up Sarah's arm. 'You and I have a little assignation,' she purred. 'Come with me.'

Sarah stiffened and glanced up at Doctor Casswell for some kind of confirmation. He inclined his head towards her, eyes bright and hawkish.

'Do as Amelia says.'

Sarah's senses were reeling, but without a word she followed Amelia across the now crowded room. She noticed Chang, a shadowy figure hovering in the background, slip away. She wondered if his leaving signified anything. But before she could ponder any further Amelia gripped her hand and guided her towards a slightly raised platform.

Sarah gasped. 'What are you going to do?'

Amelia laughed. 'Not me, darling… us. Just trust me, you'll love it. You and I are the cabaret tonight, my precious. Just relax and let yourself go.'

As soon as the light went on above the stage the conversation faded to a low hum and Casswell settled himself against one of the pillars that overlooked the circular dais. A spotlight picked out Amelia, who was standing in front of the stage, looking gorgeous in her blue silk corset.

The volume of the music rose a little, picking out a seductive Middle Eastern rhythm, and Amelia thrust her pelvis forward dramatically, while with one finger she teased at the plump lips of her naked pussy. With the other hand she stretched out and picked up a whip from the stage, and as her finger found the tight bud of her clitoris she cracked it like a thunderbolt, threw back her head, and howled like a wolf.

Casswell allowed himself a wry smile; Amelia really was a natural exhibitionist. The lithe blonde leapt up onto the stage and prowled back and forth. Sarah was watching the performance, completely stunned, open-mouthed with shock, as the beauty stalked around cracking the whip. There was a chair, over which hung a pair of handcuffs.

As the spellbound audience watched, Amelia suddenly leapt down and grabbed the unsuspecting Sarah. The girl protested and squirmed instinctively, fighting to free herself as she was relentlessly dragged onto the stage. As they struggled their way into the spotlight, Amelia seized the top of Sarah's feather-trimmed bodice and with a single violent tug she ripped it down, revealing the milky white curves of Sarah's breasts to the appreciative gathering.

There was a murmur of approval from all sides as Sarah's tormentor cupped one firm breast in her gloved fingers and squeezed it lovingly, tweaking the ripe pink nipple. Sarah sobbed and writhed miserably, but Amelia had no intention of letting up. She guided the weakening girl to the chair, her clever fingers continually working on her body and ripping away the remainder of her exquisite costume. Sarah still struggled, but less vehemently, naked now except for her shoes and stockings, and the feather mask.

Casswell sipped his champagne, impressed by their performance. He could sense the growing excitement, not just from Amelia, but Sarah too. The slim blonde threw her new slave onto the floor and then thrust her hips forward, a gloved finger teasing at her quim, holding the lips open.

Sarah cried out her revulsion, whimpering in protest while Casswell stared with pleasure, feeling the heat and excitement rising from deep within.

'No, no, please,' Sarah sobbed, her voice echoing around the enrapt audience in the garden room, but Amelia was without mercy. She caught hold of Sarah's hair and pulled her flushed face into her groin.

Sarah emitted a stifled sob of angst, trying to push herself away, and then she knew it was hopeless and surrendered, like a broken animal.

From his vantage point Rigel Casswell could not see exactly what Sarah Morgan was doing to her new mistress. But he could hear the wet mesmeric sounds of her tongue lapping at the blonde's body, and he could see the way Amelia's breasts swelled and her fingers curled in her slave's hair as she closed her eyes and sighed deeply.

He could almost feel the tendrils of pleasure creeping up through the two lovely females. Amelia threw back her head and began to move in earnest, rhythmically, grinding her hips forward in time with the increasingly competent caresses of the tongue and lips between her legs. Amelia whimpered, pulled Sarah even closer, and trailed the tip of the whip across Sarah's back as she moved.

Casswell could see Amelia's orgasm approaching. But at the very final moment she tore herself away from Sarah's tongue and lips and dragged her to her feet. With a single smooth movement she turned Sarah around, encouraged her to straddle the chair, and instantly snapped the handcuffs on, securing her tightly to the frame.

To Casswell's delight Sarah could no longer sustain the pretence of real fear; her eyes sparkled with anticipation and her flesh glowed with an inner fire. Behind her the corset clad Amelia flexed the whip speculatively and let the end cut through the air. Although only a practice swing, it made Sarah jump and stiffen.

Sarah remained motionless and waited, her eyes wide. The second swing was closer, slicing with an irresistible hiss through the cigar smoke that hung and swirled heavily around them. Casswell glanced around and smiled; every pair of eyes in the room was transfixed on the spotlit stage.

He saw Sarah tense a split second before the next stroke hit her squarely across the shoulders. And then she screamed. It was a scream that came from the pit; a desperate animal cry of pain. Her body jerked, those deliciously ripe breasts thrusting forward, her nipples stiffening visibly.

Casswell could see, framed by the wooden arc of the chair's curved back, the open lips of Sarah's sex. They glistened succulently under the spotlight's single penetrating eye.

Amelia twisted and applied the next cruel stroke.

The blow was lower this time, making Sarah's legs and pelvis surge forward wildly, pressing fiercely against the chair. Her face was contorted into an ecstatic grimace, while her hips thrust forward again, offering her sex to the audience like a ripe fruit. Mesmerised by the spectacle, Casswell's mouth was watering from the sheer erotic charge of the image the two women created.

Sarah was breathing hard, trying to retain some shred of control. And then the whip swept down again and her

220

head jerked back. Amelia smiled from under the silken mask – her teeth pearly-white and feline – and then she planted a kiss on her victim's gasping lips.

Around him, Casswell could feel the erotic temperatures rising, the guests and their slaves willing their way towards release as a single body. He counted the blows in his head.

Four… Five…

The whip cracked out again and again. By now Sarah had surrendered entirely to the compulsive beat of the explosive pain. Casswell shivered as he imagined the raw kiss of the leather cutting into her back

Six… Seven…

Sarah pressed forward, straining and desperate; desperate to avoid the hateful whip, and desperate to feel its delicious cut.

Eight… Nine…

Casswell wondered how much longer Sarah's beating could continue. The atmosphere in the garden room was strung as tight as a piano wire.

Ten—!

It was a final and decisive blow that cracked out around the crowded room and reverberated through Sarah's sweating body like a pistol shot. As if she knew it was the last stroke, she fell forward, sobbing, struggling to fill her burning lungs with rasping breaths.

Amelia, herself perspiring heavily from her efforts, dropped the whip to the stage and undid her victim's handcuffs, then dropping onto her hands and knees she crawled across the stage. The submissive pose was completely at odds with the dominant scenario that preceded it.

Casswell assumed the entertainment was over and

looked away for some more champagne, just as a man in a long dressing gown stepped up onto the stage beside the two girls. He looked back, and realised it was Oliver Turner. Amelia slithered across the stage and rubbed against her master's legs; a feline whose every move dripped with sexual promise.

From the audience came a low murmur of recognition and approval, and even for a second or two the briefest flurry of applause. Their host smiled with all the warmth of a basking shark, and stroked Amelia's pale blonde locks. She purred with delight and, still nosing and rubbing herself against his thighs, unfastened his red brocade robe. It fell open to reveal that Turner was naked beneath, his penis already erect and jutting out from his groin. Under the spotlight he looked far more impressively endowed than Casswell knew him to be.

Amelia cradled his phallus in her fingers and began to suckle at the end where a single tear of excitement glistened. She sucked greedily, hungry to pleasure him, while her other hand cupped and caressed his heavily distended scrotum. Moans of intense delight trickled out from the junction where her lips stretched around his cock.

The lithe blonde uncurled and opened her legs, a hand working its way between her thighs, long fingers dipping down into the wet ripe confines of her own sex, then rising again to smear Turner's cock and balls with her aromatic juices. Through it all the elderly gentleman's expression remained stoically impassive.

Casswell glanced around the stage. A few feet away from Oliver and Amelia, Sarah Morgan sat in the shadows, only her eyes betraying her passion, as bright as flares in the enveloping darkness. He wondered what